Freezer Burn

Joe R. Lansdale is the author of over two hundred short stories and a dozen novels, and has edited several anthologies of dark suspense and western fiction. He has won the British Fantasy Award, the American Mystery Award and five Bram Stoker Awards. He lives in East Texas with his wife and children.

Visit Joe R. Lansdale's website at *www.joerlansdale.com*

D1642698

By Joe R. Lansdale

Freezer Burn

JOE R. LANSDALE

VICTOR GOLLANCZ

LONDON

Copyright © Joe R. Lansdale 1999

All rights reserved

The right of Joe R. Lansdale to be identified as the author of
this work has been asserted by him in accordance with the Copyright,
Designs and Patents Act 1988.

First published in Great Britain in 1999
by Victor Gollancz
An imprint of Orion Books Ltd
Orion House, 5 Upper St Martin's Lane,
London WC2H 9EA

A CIP catalogue record for this book is available
from the British Library

Typeset by Deltatype Ltd, Birkenhead Merseyside
Printed and bound in Great Britain by
Clays Ltd, St Ives plc

Dedicated to the memory of Tomi Lewis.
Sleep gentle, my dear.

All comic novels that are any good must be about matters of life and death.
                    Flannery O'Connor
                    (on the writing of *Wise Blood*)

There's a guy in No. 7 that murdered his brother, and says he didn't really do it, his subconscious did it. I asked him what he meant, and he says you got two selves, one that you know about and the other that you don't know.
                    James M. Cain
                    (*The Postman Always Rings Twice*)

PART ONE

The Heist

One

Bill Roberts decided to rob the firecracker stand on account he didn't have a job and not a nickel's worth of money and his mother was dead and kind of freeze-dried in her bedroom.

Well, not completely freeze-dried. Actually, she stunk, but she seemed to be holding her own, having only partially melted into the mattress, and if he kept the door closed and pointed a fan that way to blow back the smell, it wasn't so bad.

The firecracker stand was out on the highway, and it was the week of the Fourth of July, and the stand stayed open reasonably late every night, so after a couple nights watching, seeing lots of people out there buying firecrackers, Bill decided it was a good place to heist.

He figured he ought to hit it kind of late in the night so there'd be plenty of money. He thought he might steal a few firecrackers too. He liked the teepee-shaped kind that spewed sparkles of colors all over the place, then finished by blowing up. Those were his favorites by far, and he thought if the stand had any, he might just take some, and if they didn't have any, he thought some Black Cats and some Roman candles would do.

The stand was almost directly across the highway from where he lived with his mother's body, so he didn't want to just walk over and rob it, and he didn't want to drive his car over there either, 'cause he figured someone sitting there all day in the stand looking across the highway might have noticed it parked under the sweet gum tree next to the house, and if they did, and he drove over there and robbed the stand, sure as shit, someone would remember his car. It didn't take a brain surgeon to figure that one.

Bill began to consider the angles.

One angle he was sure of was, now that his mother had died at the age of about ten million, there wouldn't be any more checks signed by her for cashing. He had practiced writing her name until he had worn out about a half dozen ballpoint pens, but never could feel confident about the way he put it down. The checks had started to stack up now, all the way to seven, and he didn't think he could get away with forgery. His mother had relished a distinct style in penmanship that only a chicken scratching in cow shit might duplicate with authenticity.

The old gal had been right enough and mean enough six months earlier, but one night, after watching Championship Wrestling, perhaps due to excitement over a particularly heated contest, or an overly vigorous inhalement of gummy bears, which she stuffed into her bony body as if they were the fruit of life, she had gone to bed and hadn't gotten up again.

Bill thought at first he ought to report it. Then it came to him that if he did he'd lose the house and wouldn't have any place to live. His mother owned everything, and except for a bit she doled out to him on check-cashing day, providing him with a roof and food to eat, there was nothing else. She hadn't left anything to him in her will. She had donated it all to some kind of veterinarian research thing so cats could be saved from bad livers or some such shit.

Frankly, Bill didn't give a flying damn about a bunch of cat livers or any part of a cat. The little bastards could die for all he cared. He'd certainly taken care of all his mother's cats after her death. Unless the fuckers had sprouted gills, or had scissors to get out of those rock-weighted tow sacks he put them in, he figured they were resting pleasantly at the bottom of the Sabine River. No liver trouble, no problems whatsoever.

No, he didn't think he ought to call the authorities and tell them his mother was dead. It seemed wiser to turn up the air conditioner in her room and keep that fan blowing and be quiet. Only thing was, now the electricity bill had come twice, then a notice, and then it had been cut off, and with no juice Mama began to stink something furious. He put a big black trash bag over her feet, up to her waist, and pulled one over her head, tied them together where they met at the waist with one of her robe belts. But that didn't hold the stink in worth a damn. He poured a whole bottle of Brut cologne over her, and that helped some. She smelled like a sixteen-year-old boy on his way to his first date.

Finally the cologne fermented with Mama and gave off an even more intense aroma. But eventually that passed. Between all the air-conditioning, the Baggies, the heat, and the stale air, the old gal semi-mummified. Not so much she didn't still smell dead, but enough it didn't run him out of the house anymore. It was now like a dog had died under the porch and was almost rotted away.

Worse than the odor was the lack of electricity. All the food in the refrigerator had spoiled and he had to sit in the dark at night and smoke his mother's cigarettes and look at a dead TV set and eat vegetables out of cans. There were plenty of cans, but he didn't really want any of it. There were goddamn beets, and goddamn green beans, and goddamn corn, and goddamn new potatoes. Not a shred of meat, except for some Beenie-Weenies, and he'd jumped on those scamps two days after the old lady bit the big one. So now it was nothing but canned vegetables, and they were running low and he'd foolishly pushed the beets back until the last, so now that's all he had to eat. Beets. He wished he'd doled those boogers out.

Sometimes he sat on the front porch with his can of vegetables and watched bugs fly across the light of the moon, and sometimes he just sat and watched people pull up at the stand across the highway and buy firecrackers. He started counting the people and figuring from the size of their sacks about how much they were spending, and that got him thinking about how much was back there in the stand each night before they closed and took it home.

Each day, as it got closer to the Fourth of July, the traffic increased. He thought if he waited until the Fourth to hit the place that would be the biggest night, and he might clean up good. He thought maybe he did, he could pay the electric bill, phone, all the rest, and manage to pay the water bill before it got turned off. It was the one thing that he'd had enough cash to pay, and he'd kept it up, but he couldn't afford it again. He was down to his last few dollars and he knew he'd miss that water. He liked to take baths, even if they were cold, and drink lots of water to keep from thinking about eating. He had paid the post office box bill for a year so he wouldn't have to worry about the mailman coming around. Not that he did any more than stuff mail in the box out by the highway, but he figured the less people he could have near the house the better, just in case he was so used to Mama that others might be able to get a sniff of her all the way out to the mailbox.

Since his mother didn't have any family other than him that would have anything to do with her, and she didn't have any friends, he figured he might could go on indefinitely, provided he learned to sign her checks or found someone willing to do it for a little cut of the money.

'Course, that plan had limits. After a bit, Social Security might figure out his Mama wasn't over a hundred years old and still living. But since she was in her eighties when she died, he thought he might could get ten years out of her checks before anyone got wise and came around to throw her an Oldest Person In America birthday party. By then, he'd have plans. Like Butch Cassidy and the Sundance Kid, he might go off to Bolivia.

The whole thing, trying to figure out what to do, made Bill's head hurt. But one thing he was certain of, a good place to start was knocking over that firecracker stand.

He thought of a couple fellas he knew might be up for the job, and though he wasn't big on cutting them in, the idea of doing it alone didn't appeal to him. Besides, they needed a getaway car, and Chaplin, one of the fellas he was thinking about, could hot-wire a waffle iron he took a mind to. And Fat Boy Wilson could drive a waffle iron if that's all they had to drive.

A few days later after all this considering, Bill drove into town on the last of his gas and found Chaplin and Fat Boy working on a car in Fat Boy's garage. Chaplin was under it and having Fat Boy pass down wrenches.

"How's the boy?" Fat Boy asked Bill.

"I'm fine. That Chaplin under there?"

"Naw, I'm Raquel Welch," Chaplin called from beneath the car, "and I'm givin' the car a blow job. How you doin'?"

"Okay."

"How's your mom, Bill?"

"Fine. Who's Raquel Welch?"

"One of the big-tittie actresses. She's a little long in the tooth now, I reckon. Hell, she might be dead."

"That don't matter none to Chaplin," Fat Boy said. "Long as her titties ain't rotted off and there's some kind of hole in her."

They laughed. Bill said, "You boys want to do a little somethin'? You know, a little job."

"You don't mean illegal, do you?" Fat Boy said. "I mean, I don't do nothing illegal."

All three laughed, and Chaplin, who had been lying on a wheeled board, a creeper he called it, slid out from under the car and got a rag and wiped his hands.

"Well," Chaplin said, "it illegal?"

"Yeah," Bill said, "it's some illegal."

"Long as it ain't killin' nobody," Fat Boy said.

"We're gonna have to have guns, but that's just for show."

"Man, I don't know," Fat Boy said. "I did that filling station over in Center with you, and you're kind of nervous when there's guns. Chaplin, he likes guns too much. I thought we might end up shootin' someone. I don't want to shoot no one. I mean, they're gonna shoot me, I might shoot 'em, but I don't want to shoot nobody I don't have to."

"You don't got to shoot anybody," Bill said. "I don't want anyone to get hurt. It's just for show."

"I might shoot somebody, it's worth the money," Chaplin said.

"It's a firecracker stand," Bill said. "I figure they take in several thousand a day. I'm sayin' we split it three ways."

"How many guys run the stand?" Fat Boy asked.

"One most of the time. Sometimes two. We hit it at closing time, take the money and run. Piece of cake. We'll need to heist a car to do the job, ditch it somewhere, have our own waitin'. We wear masks. We don't say much. We wave a pistol around. We get the money and we're gone."

"Them firecracker stands," Fat Boy said, "they're out of the city, easy targets."

"It'd be a whole lot easier than a convenience store," Chaplin said.

"That's right," Bill said. "This one is across from my house. Easy pickin's."

Two

And so it came to pass that on the Fourth of July, minutes before ten o'clock at night, which was when the stand closed, Fat Boy at the wheel of a stolen white Chevy, Bill to his right, and Chaplin in the back seat, arrived at the firecracker stand.

Fat Boy stayed in the car. Bill and Chaplin got out and went over to the stand wearing Lone Ranger style masks. A fat woman in a muumuu big enough to make a bedspread for most of Bangladesh to lie down on and wrestle a little bit, was buying some Roman candles, some punks, and some matches.

"I just love these here Roman candles," she said. "You get out where it's real dark and set 'em off, they're just as pretty as stars."

"Yes, ma'am," said the stand worker. The stand worker was a skinny fellow with an Adam's apple that moved a lot

10

and made him look like a snake trying to swallow a live gopher. When he spoke to the fat lady he seemed about as sincere as a hooker swearing she'd never let anyone come in her mouth before.

The fat lady looked at Bill and Chaplin in their masks. She said, "Boys, it's the Fourth, not Halloween."

"Yes, ma'am," Bill said. "We just think we look good in 'em."

"Well, you don't."

"Yeah, and you're fat as a fuckin' whale too," Chaplin said.

"Well, I never," she said, and got her bag of goods and waddled off to her car and wedged herself inside with a grunt and drove off. Now only Bill and his comrades and the firecracker stand worker were on the site.

The stand worker said, "I ever got that fat, I'd want someone to shoot me, skin me, and tack me on the side of a barn for target practice."

"Uh huh," Bill said. "Give me some of them Roman candles there. And a bunch of them Black Cats."

"How many's a bunch?" asked the stand worker.

"Two of them long packs," Bill said.

"Y'all come from some kind of party?" asked the stand worker.

"Somethin' like that," Bill said.

The stand worker went at gathering Bill's order. When he finished, he placed them on the counter. Bill pulled out a pistol and pointed it at him. "While you're at it, why don't you just put all your money on the counter too. I'd prefer it in a bag."

"Why you piece of shit," said the stand worker.

"Watch your mouth," said Chaplin, taking out his revolver, "or you'll find it on the other side of your head."

11

"Easy," Bill said.

"This here is my firecracker stand. What I make here is all I get, 'cept for some little farm jobs I take now and then. I ain't got a steady job. And you didn't come from no party neither."

"We crawled out of that fat lady's ass when she wasn't looking," Chaplin said.

"Pieces of shit," the stand worker said. "Pieces of shit. That's what y'all are. You're robbin' a man needs all he can get and you don't even care. There's niggers wouldn't do this to me."

"You're breakin' my goddamn heart," Chaplin said.

"Put the money on the counter," Bill said.

The stand worker gave Bill a defiant look, reached under the counter and came up with a metal box and opened it and took out the money and put it on the counter. "Get your own sack," he said.

"You give us a sack," Bill said, "and put them candles and 'crackers in there too, and if you got any of them little teepee things that spew colors and blow up, put some of them in there, or I'm gonna shoot your dick off."

At that moment, the elastic on Bill's mask gave out. The mask sprang forward and floated down and landed on the counter in front of the stand worker. But the stand worker didn't look at the mask. He looked at Bill's face.

"Hell, I've seen you before," said the stand worker, proud of himself. "You live across the road there? Yeah. You do. I know you."

Bill looked at Chaplin. Chaplin and Bill looked at the stand owner, who suddenly grew pale.

"You fucked up," said Chaplin.

"Don't," Bill said, but Chaplin shot the stand owner between the eyes. The stand owner did a short hop backwards, coiled down over his legs as if they were boneless, and lay behind the counter with his head on his knee, one hand reaching up and pulling down a box of firecrackers. Then he was still as the dirt beneath him.

"Oh my God," Bill said. "You shot him."

"He knew who you were."

"I didn't want nobody killed."

"Pray over him a bit, maybe he'll come around."

Bumfuzzled, Bill stood still as a post.

"Climb over there and get the money," Chaplin said.

Bill climbed over the counter, got a bag and shoved the money into it, got another bag and put the candles and the 'crackers in it, picked him out a few cherry bombs and the teepee things, put those in the sack. He looked through the dead man's pockets and found a quarter. He climbed over the counter, tossed the firecracker bag to Chaplin, and they darted out to the car, got in the back seat.

"I heard you shoot," Fat Boy said. "You shot him, didn't you?"

"Weren't no choice," Chaplin said.

"I didn't mean for nothing like that to happen," Bill said.

"That's what I hate about jobs where you got to have guns," Fat Boy said. "I hate it." Fat Boy drove off peeling rubber. "I hate it big. I knew someone was gonna get shot."

"Well," Chaplin said, "it weren't you, so that's good."

"It ain't good," Fat Boy said. "It ain't good at all."

"It don't matter now," Chaplin said, counting the money. "Goddamn, we got maybe three thousand dollars here."

At that moment there was a loud explosion and the car's rear end did a quick dodge to the right, went off the road

13

and into a ditch, turned over and righted again next to the woods.

Bill licked blood off his mouth and let his stomach fall back down to its proper place. He had taken a bite out of the seat in front of him, but all his teeth were still intact, and his tongue wasn't bit in two. He only had mashed his lips.

Chaplin sat next to him, very still. The sack with the Roman candles had been in front of Chaplin, and the wreck had driven him forward into one of them; it had fitted itself snugly into his eye socket. He was bent at the waist with the candle in his eye. He had one hand on the candle as if to pull it out, but he hadn't lived long enough. Blood ran along the candle and down over his hands and spilled into his lap and onto the car seat.

Fat Boy, who had a split bloody nose and a knot on his forehead big enough to wear a hat, turned in his seat, held his head, and looked at Chaplin.

"Shit!" he said. "Shit!"

Bill opened the door, stumbled out and fell down. Fat Boy got out. He leaned against the side of the car. He said, "Blowout. Fuckin' tire blew out. Dumb shit Chaplin could have stole a better car."

Bill fell down and lay on the grass for a moment, then got up. He used his pocketknife and a few hard kicks to open the trunk, pulled out the jack, the tire iron, and the spare.

"What you doin'?" Fat Boy said.

"What's it look like?"

"Chaplin's dead!"

"He ain't gonna get no more alive if we leave the tire flat. We got to get out of here."

Bill put on the emergency brake and set to work jacking

14

up the bumper to get at the blown tire. It was a real job in the dark and Fat Boy continued to wander about the car like a lost duck. He seemed to want to go somewhere but couldn't quite figure which direction to take.

"Get your ass over here and help with these lug bolts," Bill said.

Fat Boy lumbered over and got the lug wrench and went at it. He worked the bolts loose, popped two of his knuckles open in the process, pulled the tire off. Bill slipped on the spare. Fat Boy screwed down the bolts and Bill lowered the wheel and Fat Boy tightened them. Bill rolled the bad tire off into the woods and tightened down the trunk lid with a piece of a coat hanger he found back there. They got in the crumpled car, Bill on the passenger side now, and Fat Boy drove them out of there.

Three

They drove along the highway very fast and passed a deputy sheriff's car running emergency lights and siren.

"Shit," Fat Boy said. "Is that for us?"

"Got to be. Or at least for the shooting. Someone must have heard it and called. You think anyone could have seen us in the dark?"

"Ain't that dark," Fat Boy said. "And the stand had lights. We got to hide this car."

"Can't we dump it near your car?"

"Too far away. In a minute them cops'll be on our ass like hemorrhoids."

Fat Boy found a little road to the right and took it, drove down into the thick woods. The headbeams showed sparkles to the left and right. Bill realized there was water in the woods.

"Where the hell are we?" Bill said.

16

"I ain't never been down here," Fat Boy said. "But I know it's the bottoms. I know some niggers fish down here all the time. They say you get down in here good, ain't nobody ever gonna find you. There's supposed to be enough bodies down here, you could dig them all up and count 'em, there'd be enough to fill a town."

Fat Boy threw an eye on the rearview mirror, said, "Fuck!"

Bill looked over his shoulder.

Lights flashing. A moment later, sirens. Chaplin's body bounced around the back seat like a jumping bean, the Roman candle sticking out of his face, his dead hand clutching it as if holding a telescope to his eye.

"Goddamn," Fat Boy said. "Cop turned around. Someone must have given them a make on the car."

"Probably one of my nosy neighbors 'cross the highway," Bill said. "Show them fuckers you know how to drive."

Fat Boy put his foot to the floor. The car leaped. A curve showed up in the headlights, Fat Boy made it, threw dirt as he went. The dirt reflected in the red taillights like a bloody mist. In the back seat, Chaplin hopped about as if excited.

The cop car made the turn too. When Bill looked back the cop car was rocking left and right, but it fell in line and jumped close to them.

"Go! Go! Go!" Bill yelled.

There was a big curve coming up. Fat Boy went around it, pedal to the metal, nose forward, ears back, balls sucked up tight as mad baby fists.

They made the curve and the cop didn't. His car went through a barbed wire fence and smacked a tree. The front turned butter soft and looked like an accordion. Steam hissed out from under the crumpled hood and made a white mushroom cloud.

Just as they approached another curve, Bill looked back and was amazed to see the cop car back away from the tree and onto the road. It wasn't exactly motoring like it had a rocket in its ass, but it was coming. The hood flapped up and down like a gossip's tongue.

"He ain't got a prayer and a sandwich now," Fat Boy said, laughed, and they made the curve. Then there was a clunk and a grind and a bumpty-bumpty, bumpty-bump.

Fat Boy said, "Goddamn muffler's hangin'. But we ain't gonna let that stop us."

Around another curve they went, and the muffler swung to the left and came loose. But not before the rear tire met it and the muffler snapped and the end of it drove into the rubber and the tire blew. The Chevy, going about eighty, spun around in the road and left it, knocked through a barbed wire fence, rampaged over a few small trees, slapped the hell out of a couple of unsuspecting frogs, then sailed out into the water.

It was odd the way that car went in. All white and shiny, spinning around and around, almost levitating across the top of the water, then suddenly it nosed down fast. Then, as if it were a cork, it bobbed in the swamp a moment next to a blackened cypress stump.

Creatures in the water and the woods moved. The car gave off steam. The water rippled way out from the impact and frogs croaked and hopped away. The moon's image lay full and huge on the swampy water, as if God had dropped a greasy dinner plate. Inside, Chaplin had been tossed over the seat to join Bill and Fat Boy. Bill pushed Chaplin aside, put his foot on the corpse's head, climbed over the seat, and rolled down a back window as the Chevy began to slide into the gloom.

Bill climbed out. Fat Boy, wearing a steering wheel tattoo on his forehead next to the mountainous knot he had acquired earlier, fought the floating body of Chaplin off, and followed.

Moments after they abandoned the Chevy, the car went down, along with the firecrackers, the money, and Chaplin.

Bill and Fat Boy swam in the warm water. The water was thick as good beef stew. Underwater weeds and vines grabbed at their ankles and tried to hold them. They swam back toward the road. But as they did, the injured deputy's car, hissing smoke from under its hood, pulled up and stopped and the deputy, his cowboy hat twisted to one side on his head, got out, pulled a pistol, and started shooting at them.

Bill and Fat Boy turned and swam and clawed in the other direction. The shots hopped all around them, like corn popping. They kept swimming, made some thick grass that grew high out of the water, grabbed hold of it and pulled themselves into a maze of cattails, then onto a spur of land and into a nest of trees.

The deputy had reloaded and was firing again. Lead danced across the water, but after a moment, Bill and Fat Boy realized the lead was only dancing so far.

"We're out of range," Fat Boy said.

At that moment, the deputy waded into the water and started calling them "cocksuckers." They could hear his voice loud and clear across the water. He was wading and holding the hand with the pistol up out of the water and firing toward them. "Cocksuckers!" he kept saying over and over.

Before the deputy could bring them into range, they

turned and went through the trees, back into waist-high water, and started wading toward an isle where great roots stuck out from the shore and plunged into the water like anacondas frozen on film. On the island itself, gnarly willows twisted amongst cypress stumps. There were high weeds beyond that and more cattails and thick brush and plenty of darkness.

The swamp smelled like an outhouse, and the moonlight on the water made it silver. In spots near the shore the water boiled, and pretty soon they were close to the boiling, and Bill could see there were little heads sticking out of the water, and the moonlight caught the dead eyes planted on the little heads and made them no brighter, but showed them for what they were. The flat black eyes of the devil, multiplied and trapped in the triangular-shaped faces of about twenty-five cottonmouth water moccasins.

"By Jesus's blue-veined dick!" Fat Boy yelled.

Bill backpedaled, trying to return to the bank behind him. Then he heard, "Cocksuckers . . . Cocksuckers," and the water grew hot with pistol shot. Bill floundered back toward the snakes and to the right, and Fat Boy panicked, screamed, began to slap at the water to scare the snakes. But the snakes didn't scare. The slapping excited them. They swam toward Fat Boy, their heads standing out of the swamp like malignant periscopes.

Fat Boy ducked under the water, possibly trying to swim under the snakes, or hoping the old story about how snakes couldn't bite underwater was true, but the snakes dove down after him, and in the next moment he rose up wearing several of them, dispelling the myth. He screamed and screamed and the snakes struck up and out of the water and buried their fangs in him.

Fat Boy quit fighting them. He swam toward shore with

the snakes dangling from his body. He made the bank by taking hold of a root and pulling himself up. Just before he was completely on shore, the deputy yelled "Cocksucker" again, and fired, and perhaps by accident, put a load in Fat Boy's back.

Bill, who had made shore, was watching Fat Boy from behind the cypress stump. Fat Boy crawled onto shore and the snakes let go and bit him again and slithered away into the water. Fat Boy rolled onto his back and lay beneath willow shadows and a rich slice of lime-colored moonlight on his face.

The deputy, who was halfway across, partly wading, partly swimming, saw the little heads coming his way, gave out with a couple more "cocksuckers" and retreated. He made the shore ahead of the snakes and snapped a half dozen bullets across the water into the woods where Fat Boy lay and Bill cowered. He just kept firing and reloading, and Bill realized the deputy actually had two pistols. However, his marksmanship proved no better than his language, and Bill was certain the shot that had caught Fat Boy was an accident.

The deputy began to snap an empty revolver at them. He yelled. "Cocksuckers. I'm gonna get the shotgun. Hear me cocksuckers!" Then the deputy moved out of their sight, and Bill could hear him across the way, cussing and thrashing through the water back to his car.

Bill came out from behind the stump and looked at Fat Boy. Fat Boy had a head like a watermelon now. He looked much fatter all over and the steering wheel indentation and the knot made him look like some kind of space monster.

Fat Boy turned his head toward Bill. Fat Boy's eyes were barely visible. His face had puffed up all around them. Fat

Boy said, "One of 'em bit me on the balls. You got to get the poison out."

"They bit you all over," Bill said.

"But one bit me on the balls."

"It don't matter where they bit you. They bit you all over. You got shot too."

"But one bit me on the balls. Oh shit. I ain't gonna make it." Then Fat Boy's eyes went as flat and black as the eyes of the water moccasins. A cloud moved over the moon.

Four

The moon stayed behind clouds for a while, and Bill left Fat Boy where he lay and struck out into the swamp water. He felt like a sewer rat wading through a shit-clogged drain. The swamp seemed to rise up out of nowhere. One moment you were walking on land, the next you were up to your neck in water and grass and maybe water moccasins.

Bill tried not to think about the water moccasins. He understood how Fat Boy had felt about being bit on the balls. You got to go, you don't want to get it in the balls. The Old Man had told him once you could do a lot of things, but you shouldn't let nobody get their hands on your balls. Bill was uncertain if this had been street fighting or sexual advice. It was about the only real advice his father had ever given him, because when Bill was twelve the Old Man did a fade. Considering the Old Man had to deal with Bill's

23

mother all the time, it left the boy with less hurt and a world of understanding. Actually, he was proud of the Old Man for bailing. He had never had the guts to leave. He had to wait until his mother left him. It felt odd now not to be bossed about by an overbearing woman. He had grown so accustomed to it, he thought it was natural, like trips to the bathroom.

Bill heard something slither by him in the water. His bowels loosened, but he kept wading. Soon the clouds around the moon faded or rolled away, leaving only tufts of mist across its face, like an adolescent wearing cotton whiskers.

Eventually Bill climbed on a little island and lay down to rest. He could hear things moving around him in the brush and among the willows and the old cypress stumps that had once been great trees but had been cut out years ago. He could hear something else.

"Cocksucker! Cocksucker! Cocksucker!" drifted over the swamp water as clear and clean as if shouted through a bullhorn. The bastard was nuts. Maybe when he wrecked he'd banged his head and sort of lost it. Bill remembered what the deputy had said about going back to his car to get his shotgun. It was Bill's guess that if the deputy had the ammunition, he had reloaded both pistols as well.

Bill lifted up and peered in the direction he thought the last "Cocksucker!" had come from. A light was dancing in the darkness amidst the willows and cattails. The deputy had gotten a flashlight. But there was no way the bastard could be following him. You couldn't follow anyone in this muck. The sonofabitch was just lucky. Or maybe the deputy was pursuing the most logical path . . . the little islands situated between patches of swamp water.

Crawling on his hands and knees, sweating so badly his

face felt as if it had been buttered, Bill crossed the narrow little strip of land and slithered off into the water on the other side like a moccasin himself. He swam hard, but as quietly as he could, out to the center of the swamp and got hold of a cypress stump with a hole in it. While he was clinging to it, in the moonlight, he saw eyes looking out of the hollow at him. The stump was the home of a possum. The possum bared its fangs. Bill moved around to the other side of the stump and got up close to it and hoped for the best.

Out on the surface of the water he could see the heads of moccasins crossing toward the isle he had just vacated. He could hear the deputy crashing in the water and cussing a blue streak. The moccasins, perhaps offended by such language, turned, and headed back in the direction from which they had come.

Bill watched from the concealment of his stump as the deputy waded and made the little isle across the way, holding his shotgun over his head like a native bearer. He was still repeating "cocksucker" over and over.

In a moment, the deputy climbed onto the island across the way and cussed and thrashed through the growth there, and in the distance Bill could hear him cussing, and finally Bill swam out into the deeper part of the swamp and tried to strike out for an isle far across the way.

About halfway he became exhausted, considered just giving it up. But the sighting of a small gator changed his mind. He found he could tread water a lot longer than he thought. The gator cruised on. Invigorated, Bill began to swim, thinking about how gators liked to grab things and drag them down and stuff them in holes and let them ripen.

After a long time Bill made the isle he wanted, climbed

onto it and lay there and rested, and finally slept. When he awoke it was to daylight shining through a patch of water oak and willow trees. He was wearing a faceful of mosquitoes.

Five

The mosquitoes had enjoyed quite a feast. Bill's lips were swollen and his face wasn't feeling all that good either. It seemed as if his skin was a sack of light bulbs someone had stepped on. Bill lay there and felt the steamy heat and brought a weak hand up and slapped the mosquitoes away. They gathered back, like beggars looking for money.

Bill ran a hand over his face, was amazed to feel what the mosquitoes had done. His skin felt like some kind of craft project that involved glue, stones, dried peas, and seashells. He wobbled to his feet, walked around, found a dead calf lying in the middle of the saw grass. The little dude was covered in mud, mosquitoes, worms, ants, and flies. Bill wondered about the worms and ants. How the hell did they get on these islands? Were they like him? Fuck-ups who had ended up here with no place to go and nothing to eat but a stupid calf that had crawled through a fence after greener grass, wandered off into the swamp and died.

Now that he thought about it, he decided he wasn't like the ants or worms at all. He was more like the calf. He had struck out for greener pastures and ended up with a faceful of bug needles and an intense dose of the raw ass. And the water hadn't done his shoes any favors either. He reached down, got hold of one of the soles, discovered it was coming loose. His feet felt awful in his shoes. Squishy, lumpy, and damned uncomfortable.

Bill studied the calf, and for a moment envied the insects. Even that rotting meat looked good. He felt weak and hungry and just plain mad. He didn't have so much as a stick of gum to chew. He found himself watering up thinking of those cans of beets back at the house.

Shit, it wasn't supposed to come out this way. His mother had been right. He was stupid. She said that's why she was giving everything she owned to the cat livers, because a liver might be fixed, and he surely couldn't.

Bill let out his breath and felt sorry for himself. He'd had a batch of money in his hands and he lost it in the car. The firecrackers too. He had panicked. He hadn't even thought to grab the money on the way out of the car. The heist was at the bottom of the swamp somewhere. Monopoly money for some gator.

The mosquitoes were so fierce Bill found himself forced off the island and into the swamp water. It was deep on the other side, but he decided to go that way for no other reason than he didn't want to go backwards.

The deputy had most likely called reinforcements by now, or perhaps he was still wandering madly about in the bottoms, waving his shotgun and firing his pistols, fright-

ening the wildlife and calling everything he saw a cocksucker.

Bill waded and tried to figure his odds. He decided they
might not be too bad. Maybe someone across the way had
seen the car, but that didn't mean they had recognized
him. Even if they found Fat Boy's body, which they would,
and found Chaplin at the bottom of the swamp with a
Roman candle in his head, it didn't mean he was impli-
cated. If he could get out of the swamp and make it back
to his place, perhaps he could lay low and the whole thing
would slide by. There might be suspicions, but that wasn't
the same as facts. Maybe if he used his head he could get
to the car Fat Boy had planted. But no, that wouldn't be
smart. That belonged to Fat Boy, and he wanted to stay
away from anything like that. He tried to remember if
there was anything of his in Fat Boy's hidden car, but he
couldn't think of a thing except a Baby Ruth wrapper, and
he didn't know if that would hold fingerprints or not.
Maybe if they were smeared with chocolate. But no, he remembered now that he had thrown the wrapper out the
window. He felt good about that. Maybe things were coming out better than he had expected.

'Course, he figured he'd have to do something with
Mama, in case the cops came by to search. They might get
a lead or something, and if they didn't find anything there
to make them suspicious, he'd be all right. But a rotting
old woman in the bedroom in black plastic bags would be
a sure tip-off. He had to find a way to get rid of her. Feed
her to some dogs or something. There had to be a way.

Then again, what if he had been somehow identified and
the cops had already searched, found Mama and her
aroma? They could be lying in wait for him.

Bill went on like that for a time, his mind wandering

aimlessly from one thought to another and not clinging to any one of them in a serious fashion.

He ducked under the water and came up with a handful of mud and rubbed it on his face and the back of his neck to keep back the mosquitoes. It worked pretty well. The cloud of mosquitoes diminished, if failed to vanish.

Bill swam to a clutch of logs in the middle of the swamp and clung there. The logs were rotting and they had drifted down into this slow part of the water and were dammed up there, as if resting. In their midst, Bill could see a floating Clorox bottle with a line on it. Someone's homemade trot line most likely. He got hold of it and pulled on it to see if there might be a fish, but there wasn't even a hook. Whatever might have been hooked had long broken loose. He let the Clorox bottle go. Free of the log jam it floated out into the middle of the water and collected green moss.

After about fifteen minutes of rest, hanging on the logs, being of service to hungry mosquitoes who had discovered an unprotected spot on the crown of his head, Bill struck out again.

He made another spit of dirt, crossed it, waded, swam, and did this routine until it was high noon and he was so hungry he thought if he could bend over far enough he'd gnaw his balls off.

Finally the swamp thinned, broke, and there was a barbed wire fence and a mushy stretch of pasture. Possibly the calf's home before it wandered off in search of its fortune.

Bill started across the pasture, stepped in cow shit, saw some cows, and by late midday came to the end of the pasture and another barbed wire fence. He crossed the fence and kept walking. The ground had become more solid. He was finally getting away from the swamp and bottom land.

The mosquitoes were less thick and less insistent. He was weak and hungry and hot and his head hurt all over from the mosquito bites. He felt as if he had been beat in the face with a rake.

Eventually he came to a thin line of trees and a creek. The water was fairly clear. He got down by the side of the creek and cupped his hands and pulled water out and drank it. His tongue was swollen and hot and the water felt and tasted pretty good, but there was a coppery aftertaste.

Perhaps he had swallowed some of the swamp water and it had made him sick, or maybe he had been sleeping with his mouth open and a batch of mosquitoes had enjoyed a tongue sandwich, and all this had thrown off his taste buds.

It didn't matter. He was still thirsty, so he dipped his hand and drank more, but this time he realized the taste in his mouth was from the water.

He looked up the creek, saw there was a film in the water and the film was dark, the color of cough syrup. Bill went down the creek and around the bend and jumped back. There in the water, the top of his head blown off, his ankle stretched out and wrapped in some vines, was the deputy.

Bill squatted down and looked at him. The deputy's jaw was gone and so was the top of his head. Bill could see that somehow the deputy had tripped and the sawed-off shotgun had gone off and caught the deputy under the chin and stopped him from cussing, walking, or anything else.

At first Bill was elated, then he realized that with the deputy missing a manhunt would go out for certain. Probably there was one already with the cops combing the area for the firecracker stand robbers, and when they found this deputy, boy were they going to be mad.

'Course, that still didn't mean they knew he was in-volved. If he was careful, he might go undetected.

Bill crawled up to the other side of the creek and peeked through the thin line of trees there, saw something that surprised him.

PART TWO

Frost

Six

There was a huge pasture and the grass was cut way short and summer-burned to the color of a saltine cracker, and Bill knew if he stepped on it the grass would crackle like corn flakes. Parked on the pasture were a number of caravan-style trucks and silver trailers with brightly painted sides hooked up to semi-cabs, and there was an old station wagon and a motor home.

The trailers had pictures of weird people, wild animals, and snakes painted on them, and blazed across one in red paint was ODDITIES OF THE WORLD.

There was one shiny silver trailer off to the right, away from the others, as if placed there on special assignment. Painted on its side in black and blue was a stocky, bearded wild man encased in a block of ice. The man was blue-skinned with black hair and the ice block was a lighter blue.

Above this were the words ICE MAN written out as if in icicles.

There were a handful of people moving amongst the trailers and trucks, and even from a distance Bill could tell they were not normal folk. One was a tall lean pin-headed man in overalls and another was a woman with a beard and a green dress with some kind of dark pattern on it.

There were a number of others that Bill could not see well, and could only think of as being in various states of ugly. One actually ran on all fours, and had a spine bent like a horseshoe. A midget in a porkpie hat stood next to the bearded lady, as if ready to crawl under her dress and hide.

Bill settled down in the creek bed and looked at the dead deputy and wondered what he should do. He was surprised at how tired he was. The creek bed was cool and there was an indentation in it and the dirt was soft and damp, and without really realizing it, Bill made himself comfortable, and soon was asleep.

When Bill awoke he was famished and thirsty and none of it had been a dream. It was growing late and the sunlight had lessened, though it would be light until nine o'clock or so. Bill wondered what time it was. He went over to the deputy and checked to see if the deputy had a watch. He did.

Bill picked up the deputy's arm and pulled it out of the water and looked at the watch on the corpse's wrist. The watch was obviously waterproof. The second hand ticked away, and the time read seven forty-six.

Well I'll be screwed and tattooed, thought Bill, I've slept for hours.

Bill dropped the deputy's wrist, waded upstream away from the flow of blood from the deputy's head—which had stopped, but the idea of it still bothered him—and dipped his hand in the water and scooped out a drink. The water felt good and tasted sweet at first, but soon it made his stomach hurt.

He decided he had to find food, no matter what. It was just the sort of thing that would make him fuck up, being this hungry. He had to have something to eat, even if he had to show himself to a bunch of freaks.

Bill came out of the creek and climbed over the bank and walked toward the caravan. There weren't as many freaks as before, but he could see the guy who ran on all fours, and two that he had not seen earlier. They both appeared to have heads about the size and shape, if not the color, of jack-o'-lanterns. They were tossing a Frisbee back and forth, and the dog-man was running between them, leaping up, trying to grab the thing in his mouth. The meat heads laughed and the dog-man made a crude noise and kept at it.

Bill staggered in their direction. It was slightly warmer away from the riverbank, and Bill could see the late evening sun hanging low in the sky like a cracked fertile egg, leaking gold and yellow and blood-red chicken all over the horizon, seeping through the trees.

Scissortails darted across the sky in search of bugs, and Bill could hear cars out on the highway beyond, buzzing happily along with no concerns for lost heist money, wet Roman candles, dead deputies, or melting mothers in black plastic bags.

As Bill neared the trailers the meat heads ceased their game, paused to look at him. The dog-man didn't seem to notice, and when one of the freaks lowered the Frisbee to his side, the dog-man snatched it from his hand with his mouth, ran in a circle and leaped and came down and saw

Bill walking toward him. The Frisbee dropped from the dog-man's mouth and he pushed his head in Bill's direction, as if trying to recognize someone familiar. Bill got the impression the man might even be sniffing the air, but he was too far away to be certain.

As he grew nearer, the dog-man began to hop up and down like a mechanical pup, then bounded away in the direction of one of the trailers.

Bill didn't realize it right off, but as he neared the freaks, he discovered he had both of his hands extended, palm up, beggar position. He was so hungry and so tired, so in need of anything and everything, he couldn't help himself. He fell down twice, and pretty soon the freaks with the big heads had him under each arm and were half carrying, half dragging him toward the trailers.

Perhaps, he thought, I am an alien abductee, and a moment from now they'll have me on a cold table with salad tongs spreading my butt cheeks and a cold wet alien finger up my ass. You hear about alien abductions, the asshole is always a prime target. And they liked to jack people off for sperm. He thought he could handle that part better than the finger up the ass. It might even be kind of restful.

When they were a few feet from the trailers, the dog-man and a large fiftyish man with thick snow white hair and eyebrows housing a couple of renegade black hairs appeared.

The man wore a nice white suit, a white and yellow checkered vest, a pearl white shirt, and a bow tie that was checked to match the vest. He had on shiny white shoes and thin white socks which were visible because the pants were a smidgen too short. Little white hairs poked through the thin socks. He looked at Bill in a quizzical manner, turning his head this way and that.

The dog-man was still bouncing, and now that he was

close up, Bill could see that he was wearing gray coveralls. He had a dark elongated face that looked all the world like a dog snout, and beneath the snout there was a well-tended pencil-thin mustache. His ears had hair growing out of them, and his back legs ended in pithy nubs encased in leather bags drawn tight around his ankles. His hands were flat against the ground, and around the palm area he had wrapped some sort of padding.

The dog-man sat back on his haunches and kept repeating something over and over that Bill couldn't quite make out because the dog-man spoke as if he might have a biscuit lodged in his throat.

Weak from hunger, Bill felt himself collapsing between the arms of the bulb heads, and pretty soon he lay on his back and the sky whirled blue and gray with orange at the fringes. The bulb heads bent over him.

He heard someone say, "Give him air," and the bulb heads moved away. The face of the snow-headed man moved into his line of sight, and the man bent over him, and he felt the man's hands at his chest, unbuttoning his shirt. He began to breathe better. He rolled his head to the side and smelled the drying grass, and from that angle he could see the last of the sunlight hanging between the trees, as if a giant with an inflamed hemorrhoid was mooning him.

The dog-man was repeating himself over and over, and finally Bill realized what it was he was saying.

"One of us. One of us. One of us."

Seven

Bill had a fuse in his dick and it was being lit by the
deputy. As the fuse burned down, taking his dick with it,
nearing his balls, he knew there was going to be an explosion, but there didn't seem to be anything he could do
about it.

He just lay on his back on a little spit of land out in the
middle of the swamp swarming with water moccasins, and
couldn't move. The deputy, whose jaw was hanging by a
stringy strand of flesh, sat on a cypress stump and looked at
Bill and moved what was left of his mouth. He couldn't
make a sound, but Bill knew he was saying, over and over,
"Cocksucker. Cocksucker. Cocksucker."

Bill tried to lift his hands to put out the fuse, but nothing happened. He was confused by this. He had lifted his
hands often enough, and had certainly pulled his johnson
under some pretty difficult circumstances (such as trying to

concentrate while the smell of his dead mother floated into his bedroom from next door and stuck up in his nostrils thick as dirty cotton wads), but now, he couldn't do a thing with his thing. The fuse was almost to his balls, and when it went, well, it was going to blow him all to hell and back, and it wasn't going to do his nuts any good either.

He thought maybe he ought to let it burn down and go. Here he was, all worn out on an isle in a swamp sur- rounded by water moccasins, a dead deputy dripping his jaw on a stump nearby, and his dick burning away as he lay helpless on his back, so maybe he ought to just lie here and close his eyes and let it all go, blow him out of this life and into nothingness. What was the point of going on?

He lay there committed to doom, waiting to blow, then decided he couldn't do that. Couldn't just lie back and ex- plode into nothingness. He felt stronger suddenly, reached for his dick, found it under a sheet, then heard, "One of us," and opened his eyes.

"No, Conrad," said the white-haired man. "I don't think so. I think he's some kind of accident."

Bill considered this but couldn't figure what the man meant by that. He was lying on a bed, naked under a sheet, holding himself, and the white-haired man was reaching over to lift his head with one hand and place a cup of water to his lips with the other.

Bill looked up into the white-haired man's face. The face was somewhat fleshy and pink and the eyes were so blue they looked almost purple. The lips were pale, and there was a hint of white stubble on his upper lip and chin. There was a bright light behind the man's head, and it shined through his pale hair and around his head and looked like a halo.

Bill drank.

The dog-man, Conrad, was nearby, almost even with the edge of the bed, snuffling near the old man's elbow. Conrad lifted his head and poked it close to Bill's face. Bill rolled his head toward Conrad's strange snout and pulsating nostrils. He could see the neatly trimmed mustache, under the dog-man's nose like a trained caterpillar. He was so tired he didn't really feel surprised, disgusted, or amused. He didn't feel much of anything.

The dog-man changed his snuffling from the old man's elbow to Bill's face. "One of us," the dog-man said defiantly.

"Have it your way," said the white-haired man, lowering the cup, then lowering Bill's head onto the pillow. "How are you, son?"

Bill couldn't speak. His tongue seemed too full in his mouth. He nodded.

"Can you sign?" said the white-haired man. "I can read sign."

Bill shook his head.

Another face appeared. A young woman with short blond hair and a face sugary as a confection. She had a cute freckled nose, lips so red they looked as if they had been colored by a cherry snow cone. She was bouncy. She bent over him and he could smell her, and she smelled like fresh cut hay and wet sex and a dab of men's cologne and a sheen of healthy sweat. Her eyes were almost black and he could see himself in them.

She was wearing a man's white strap T-shirt and her round breasts swung inside it like two sweet melons in a cotton sack. She had a puzzled look on her face as she examined him.

"I think Conrad's right," she said. "I think he's one of

42

them. I betcha too, way he's all hunched up there, he's playin' with his pecker."

Bill let go of his dick and carefully slid his hand down by his side. The girl stood up and Bill rolled his head slightly. His eyes came to rest on her belly. The T-shirt did not extend that far, and her little belly button, which he noted was an outtie, not an innie, was exposed, as if inviting him to suck it. It had a ring through it and on the ring was a little jewel the color of blood.

She had on faded blue jean shorts with very little jean or shorts to them. Her legs, like the rest of her body, were smooth and tanned. She was not very tall, but at least two thirds of her appeared to be legs. The shorts fit her tight in the crotch and her pussy looked as if it might be working the zipper from the inside.

Hair fanned out from the top of the shorts, which were unbuttoned and curled open and held in place by the zipper alone. The hair thinned as it crawled up her belly and into the belly button. The hair that escaped from the shorts was darker than the hair of her head, reddish, as if formerly blond but dyed with blood, or perhaps a hint of rust.

"Just another one of your strays," said the girl.

The white-haired man looked at the woman and frowned. He turned his attention back to Bill, said, "It's all right, son, don't pay her no mind."

Bill managed to weakly shake his head.

The old man said, "I had to dispose of your clothes. They were quite soiled. But we have some that will fit you. Right now, you need rest."

"You're nothing but a sucker, Frost," Bill heard the girl's voice say.

"Yes," he answered, "I lack your Darwinistic view, I suppose."

"Hah!" the girl said.

Bill tried to speak again, but still couldn't. His tongue was like a dry sponge. The old man smiled at him and made a kind of face that told him everything was okay.

Bill stared into the white-haired man's face for a long moment, then turned in search of the blonde's belly button, and found it. He kept sight of it and the red jewel in it as long as was possible, then closed his eyes.

He fell asleep almost immediately. He didn't dream of a fuse this time. He didn't dream of the deputy with the blown-away jaw. He didn't dream of an isle in a swamp or water moccasins either.

He dreamed of laying the blonde on her back and licking her belly button, lathering up the hair below it, pulling down that zipper. From there the dream really got good.

Eight

When he awoke it was dark in the room except for one light that was by the door, and it was a weak light. It made a pool on the floor like dirty melted cheese.

Bill sat up in bed and pulled the sheet down. He was completely naked. He looked around for his clothes, but he couldn't see that well, as the light didn't extend that far.

He pulled the sheet off the bed and wrapped it around himself and wandered over to the light and discovered a chair on the other side of the door by a desk. He sat down in the chair and felt very ill. He was still hungry.

"Ah, you're better."

Bill jumped.

A shape glided into the room, a switch was flicked, and there was full light. The white-haired man was standing over him, and he leaned forward and touched Bill's forehead, then touched Bill's eyelid with his thumb, peeled it wide and looked into Bill's eye. He switched to the other eye and did the same. When he was finished he made a kind of huffing sound, said, "You look much better, son."

"Thank you," Bill said, discovering his tongue to be working.

"You can speak," said the white-haired man. "Capital. My name is Frost. John Frost. Some people call me Jack Frost but most just call me Frost. A little joke, you see. You've heard of Jack Frost, haven't you?"

"Nips your nose, or something," Bill said.

"There you are. And your name?"

"Bill."

"Good. Bill. That's easy to remember. Hungry, Bill?"

"I'll say."

Frost disappeared from the room and down a short hallway and into what served as the motor home's dining area. Bill leaned forward in his chair and watched him move around in there by the stove. Bill stood up and securely fastened the sheet about himself and went after him.

When Frost saw him, he smiled. "I have some chicken broth here. Quite good for what ails you. And I have some thick bread and cheese. I hope that will be adequate."

"Right now I could eat the ass out of a menstruatin' mule," Bill said.

Frost reddened, making him look a bit like a beardless Santa Claus. "Well," Frost said. "Well. Certainly. A mule. Yes."

Frost poured the broth from a steaming pan into a large cup and sat it in front of Bill, who had taken a seat at the dining table. He brought plates to the table, then the bread and cheese. He poured Bill and himself a glass of milk.

"Eat, boy, eat," Frost said.

Bill ate. He tried to go about it nicely, but he was too

starved. His lips were so swollen from the mosquito bites he found it was difficult to stick the food into his mouth, so he drank all the soup and ate a little of the cheese and bread. Frost gave him more soup. Bill soaked the bread and cheese in it and slurped it down noisily and drank another glass of milk.

Frost said, "I have some clothes you can wear. I'm a little heftier than you, but they should fit you all right. Loose is the fashion, they say."

"Thanks," Bill said. He studied the man carefully as he sipped his second glass of milk. He seemed genuinely kind and gentle. One of those souls you read about or see in movies, but seldom encounter. A true Good Samaritan. Bill thought this could really work out. The blonde was right. Frost was a prime sucker. Bill began to figure the angles, but soon gave it up. After all he had been through, angles were a little hard to come by.

"What you got here?" Bill asked.

"How's that?"

"This a freak show?"

"Why yes."

"I seen that dog fella. What exactly happened to him?"

"Conrad. Why, nothing happened to him, son. He was born that way. His parents abandoned him and he was raised in an orphanage and finally he ended up with me. My right-hand man, actually."

"He ain't really part dog, is he?"

"Oh, goodness no. His show name is Rex the Wonder Dog. A bit of his humor, you see. But certainly not. He's as human as you or me."

"I wonder, a guy like that, he ever get any pussy?"

Frost moved his mouth about for a moment, then took a deep breath. "Well, I don't know as I can say . . . He likes the bearded lady, but . . . Well, I just don't know . . . Had enough?"

"You got any more?"

"Sure do." Frost poured Bill another cup of soup and sat down again. "You . . . go to high school?"

"Yeah. I didn't do so good, though. I think they passed me to get rid of me."

"What's your line of work?"

"Haven't really got one right now."

"Hard to get a job?"

"I guess."

"You know, you could be at the right place."

"How's that?"

"Well, I think I should be straight with you, Bill. This is, as you said, a freak show, and you have . . . some peculiarities."

"Peculiarities?"

Frost reached across the table and touched a hand to Bill's face.

Bill reached up and touched himself. His face was strange to his fingers. He went down the hall, found the bathroom, went in there, and turned on the light and looked in the mirror.

A monster was looking back.

Nine

At first he thought perhaps he had been snake-bitten, but it made no sense. He felt okay except for being wasted, and if he had been bitten he felt he'd have known it.

Bill leaned closer to the mirror. His eyelids were huge, and his nose was knotted up, along with his forehead, which had a series of angry red welts across it like a bridge built of heated stone. Every inch of flesh on his cheeks was bloated and inflamed and itched. His lips were blowed up like inner tubes. They had rolled back on one side of his mouth to reveal his teeth.

Mosquito bites, only much worse than he had assumed. He had lain down amongst thousands of mosquitoes, and while he slept, they'd had their way with him. His face had hurt bad for a while, but now the real hurt was past and there was only the swelling and the itching, a bit of heat behind the skin. He thought he must be allergic to them.

That's what the dog-man had been talking about. One of us. One of us. He'd assumed Bill was a freak.

Wow, thought Bill, I'm disguised.

When Bill returned to the table, Frost said, "I must ask. How did you arrive here?"

"I was hitchhiking. The driver had a little accident. I banged my head, and when I awoke, well, here I was."

"Was the driver hurt?"

"I can't say. He was gone. I guess he put me out beside the road. I wandered in the woods after that."

Frost thought about that for a while. Bill couldn't tell if he was convinced by the story or not. Frost changed tactics, asked, "Your face, that isn't how you were born, is it?"

"Mosquitoes."

"What?"

"My face is swollen, that's all. Mosquito bites."

Frost let out with a whoop. "I'll be darned. Fooled even me. I've seen many a freak, and you fooled even me. I've never seen anything like it. Maybe in the daylight I would have known. I thought it was some kind of industrial accident. An explosion of some kind. Mosquitoes. Now that's the ticket. I've never known anyone to be bitten that bad before."

Bill smiled, and he knew a smile on his face must look strange and hideous. Then he quit smiling. He said: "I suppose it'll go away. Probably I'm allergic."

"Well, now, mosquito bites. I reckon it will. I suppose."

"But you're not certain?"

"It's hard to be certain of anything," Frost said.

"How do you . . . Why do you hang around all these freaks? Doesn't it . . . depress you?"

Frost smiled. "Freaks are only mistakes of nature, but

50

they have hearts and minds like everyone else. Some, like the pinheads and the balloon heads, do not have good minds, but they have feelings just the same. Suppose your face stayed that way?"

"I'd have an operation. I'd kill myself. I wouldn't live like this."

"Oh, you might. Freaks live among freaks here. We accept one another."

"But you're not a freak."

Frost smiled. "No?"

Frost stood and unbuttoned his shirt and pointed to his chest. On his left breast was a tiny gray hand, the wrist growing from the location of his heart, or at least the location one imagined for the heart. The hand poked into the air with slightly bent fingertips; the hand looked like a crustacean or prehistoric spider that had been partially boiled. The gray flesh was lined with dark, thin veins that throbbed with blood.

"There was a whole child here once," Frost said, tapping the hand. "We were both living, but I was freed of him and he was . . . destroyed. I know no other way to say it. This is all that remains. This hand. The wrist is connected to vital organs. They could not cut him all the way clear. The hand is a part of me. It beats with my pulse, with my blood. It is me, and him."

"Good God!"

"That's not all." Frost unbuttoned his pants and lowered them and scooped at his underwear and peeled them down over his ample right hip and showed a massive red scar that ran all the way up his right side. "And here was the third. Triplets. By operation and the choice of my parents, I lived, and they died. They were misshapen. I was the easiest to save. I am one of three and I am all three. Sometimes, late

51

at night, I can almost feel the hand at my chest, squeezing, trying to drive its fingers through my chest, angry I survived, wanting to mash the life from me. And the scar on my hip. It heats up, pains me. When it's cold especially. Other nights, the scar and the hand are companions."

"You were Siamese triplets?"

"Incorrect term, but as I said, I was one of three. I am still one of three. You can not create one by destroying two. Had my parents chosen for them to survive, they would have been my brothers."

"You couldn't have lived a normal life."

Frost readjusted his clothes. "True. But there's very little normal about wearing the wounds and remains of your brothers. To know I survived because I was in the middle, easier to save because my heart was stronger and my appearance normal, it has its burden."

"They didn't look right?"

"They were misshapen. Prunish is the word used to describe them. Shriveled up like little mummies. They wouldn't have grown very large, either of them, but I would have grown to the size I am now, carrying them with me. One clutched to my chest like a nursing baby, the other hanging to my hip like a pet monkey."

"Shit, you're lucky," Bill said. "You're alive and they're dead. That's no burden."

Frost's face took on a sardonic air. "You think so?"

"Take it from someone who doesn't have any luck. You're lucky."

"I suppose it's all in the way you look at things. Do you have more to tell me about why you're wandering about in the woods, hungry, worn out, and mosquito-bit?"

"I don't guess so," Bill said.

Frost studied him. "Well, I trust my instincts. You don't look like a murderer."

Bill thought: No, I look like someone with a million mosquito bites.

"I suppose you have your secrets and your reasons. You're welcome here. You may sleep in my place tonight. Tomorrow night, you wish to stay, we must find you another bed. When you feel stronger, you may leave."

"I'm much obliged, Mr. Frost."

"That's all right, Bill. That's quite all right. I'm always glad to help a man that's down. Especially one I can see needs the help. If there is one thing I believe, it is this. Man is meant to help man get along in life, and that is our singular purpose on this earth."

"Thanks," Bill said, and thought: Boy are you a dumb shit.

Ten

We got to sleep on the couch while a guy with a fucked-up face we don't even know sleeps in our bed?"

"Just for tonight. Must you curse?"

"Must I? No. But I want to."

Bill could hear them talking at the other end of the trailer. They were trying to be quiet, or at least Frost was, but their voices carried clearly into the bedroom.

Bill lay there listening to them because he couldn't sleep. He had slept too much already. He thought that was sort of funny. Just a short time before he couldn't get enough sleep, now he was wide awake with his hands behind his head looking at the ceiling, listening to the beautiful blonde tell Frost she wanted her bed back.

Bill was considering all this, pretty amazed. How in the world had this hot blonde hooked up with that freak,

Frost? Frost was a nice enough guy, but that hand on his chest, that scar on his side, it gave Bill the willies.

After listening to them awhile, Bill showered and the warm shower helped him become sleepy again. He went back to bed and fell asleep right off, but he didn't stay that way. He awoke to the door opening. He turned his head and saw framed in the moonlight the blonde. He could not really see her face, but he knew it was her because he could smell her. That wonderful smell of wet pussy and men's cologne.

Her hair lay tight against her head, and there in the shadows, except for the moonlight on her face, her shape seemed inhuman. When she turned to look in his direction he could not see her eyes, and the shadows gathered about her in such a way as to make her appear tentacled, like a great squid wearing a cap of white gold. The tentacles roiled and writhed and she shifted and the moonlight brightened as it lost a wreath of clouds and came more clearly through the windows. Suddenly she was clearly outlined in the doorway and her smell came to him more strongly than before.

She stood there for some time. He could not tell if she could see him looking at her or not. Finally she turned and gently closed the door.

Once again, Bill heard them speak. Frost called her to bed, and she said, "You done what you're supposed to do?"

"It's not necessary," said Frost.

"It is to me."

"Just this once we do different?"

"No."

"I can do it afterwards."

"There isn't going to be any afterwards, you don't do what I want."

"Very well."

A moment of long silence, then Frost again. "Now come to bed," and Bill heard movement in there, the sound of clothes dropping to the floor, a body climbing onto springs and cushions, and Bill thought: Jumpin' Jesus. She's gonna screw the freak, then he heard muted breathing, a grunt and a groan, a squeak and a cry, then all was silent and the night passed on, deep and dark and still, passed on gently into a gray morning with muted sunlight and the sound of a gentle but persistent rain tapping on the trailer.

As he lay there, wide awake in the morning, he heard movement again in the other room and he knew from the sounds that they were at it again, and Bill wondered if it was the hand on Frost's chest that turned her on, wondered if while Frost screwed her with his heavy body she would reach up and touch the little amputated hand, run her fingers over the smooth gray fingers and over the throbbing veins, and perhaps with her other hand she was reaching out to hold the scar ridge on Frost's hip.

Considering all that, Bill began to think of himself as the hand, and the thought of the blonde beneath (or above) Frost angered him, and he, the hand, began to turn his fingers down and thrust them deep into Frost's chest and grab hatefully at the old man's beating heart until it gave up its blood like juice from a mashed plum.

Eleven

Early morning Bill examined his face in the bathroom and was amazed at it. He washed it and went outside and moved about between the trailers, the rain splattering down on his head and spreading his hair and coating his scalp. It felt cool and good on his hot mosquito-bit face.

He was dressed in the clothes Frost had left for him. They fit him big, especially the pants, which he had cinched up in the waist with a belt, and shortened by rolling the cuffs slightly. He began to realize that Frost was much taller than he looked, and the old man's shoulders were wide and his chest thick. Bill wore his own shoes, and as he stood in the rain he bent his head and watched the rain clear the mud from them. When he tired of this, he watched the gray morning lighten.

As he walked among the trailers looking at the brightly painted signs on their sides, the rain went away and the sun came out and the day immediately grew hot and sticky as the crack of a fat man's ass.

Bill walked aimlessly about, came to the trailer with the picture of the Ice Man on its side. He stared at the painting for a long time, at the gnarled-looking body, at the thick black hair on the head, face, chest, and crotch. The crotch had been cleverly painted so that you could see black pubic hair, but where the tallywhacker should've been there was a painting of a swirl of frost, thick as whipping cream. An orgasmic explosion, perhaps.

Bill couldn't help but wonder if you saw the Ice Man in person, you got to see his dick or not. Was he wearing Fruit of the Looms? A jock strap? A towel? Or was he in the raw with a dick the size of an anaconda? Or maybe he had a dick like an acorn. Bill remembered a boy in his PE class like that. A great big burly sonofabitch who spent his time pushing everyone else around, and one day, in the shower, Bill saw the source of the bully's anger. He had a wart for a dick. Even hard, Bill figured that dude's hole puncher couldn't have been much bigger than a baby carrot. A thing like that could give you a pissed-off attitude.

The bully saw him seeing that, and later that day the bully pushed him around. Bill smiled at him, and they both knew what the smile was about. The bully walloped him, but after that left him alone and sometimes didn't shower, but went to class smelling like the south end of a goat, his dirty little baby pecker tucked into oversized underwear.

Bill walked around to the door of the trailer. The metal steps beneath the door were hoisted up and bolted into place. On the door there was another painting of the Ice Man. He was supposed to be lying down in his ice, but the way the painting looked, filling the door, it seemed as if the Ice Man was standing upright in a block of ice. The hair looked different in this painting, and the art was a little weak in spots, as if the painter had been in a hurry to collect his fee and get drunk. The body was hairier, and the eyes were crossed; they seemed to look at Bill no matter where he stood. It gave him the creeps.

Bill wondered what was inside the trailer. He wondered if the Ice Man was a freak. Or an act. Or if it was some kind of display made of chunks of rubber.

He ambled around the trailer and put his hand on its side. It was cold. It felt good in the East Texas muggy morning, and Bill kept his hand there for a long time, as if drawing energy from it. He leaned his face against the trailer, and that felt even better.

Finally he strolled around and came face-to-face with Rex the Wonder Dog. Or rather crotch to face. Wonder Dog was moving about on all fours.

Rex, or Conrad, was wearing red overalls and he sat back on his haunches, looking at Bill. The dog-man's shock of black hair was plastered to his head and his little mustache appeared to be oiled; it was shedding water. The hair in his ears was wet and dripping downward, like poisoned plants. At first Bill thought the Wonder Dog, like himself, had been out in the rain, but he soon realized the Wonder Dog's outfit was dry and his mustache was waxed, and that he had most likely come fresh from the shower.

Bill had a hard time envisioning that. The dog-man in the shower.

The Wonder Dog turned his head to the left and studied Bill. Bill did not like the Wonder Dog's eyes, which at one moment seemed gray, another blue, and another green. And that face, elongated like that, the lips dark and the chin nonexistent, it was creepy as a masturbating fat girl on a nude beach.

"My name is Conrad," said the Wonder Dog in his gravelly voice.

"Mine's Bill."

"Will you be staying?"

"Well, I suppose," Bill said. "For a while. Not long."

"It's not bad here," Conrad said. "Things change now and then, but all in all it's the same, and the same isn't bad."

"Yeah, well, I'll keep that in mind."

"Good," said Conrad. He raised up his back legs and dropped his arms to the ground and wandered off. Bill watched him go, surprised he had no tail.

A few minutes later the campground was buzzing. The pointy heads and the meat heads and the fat lady with the beard and some other folks with oddities Bill couldn't quite categorize were moving about. They seemed to come out of their trailers all at once. A moment later, a big kerosene stove was dragged out of one trailer by folks Bill had not seen before, a couple of black twins connected at the shoulder, with one set of legs between them. The head on the left leaned to port.

The appearance of the two made Bill think of a character on a television show he'd watched as a kid. *The Little Rascals,* it was called first, but later they changed it to *Spanky and Our Gang.* The show had been old even when he was a kid. A grown-up Buckwheat, he looked like. They looked like. Double Buckwheat.

Out of another trailer came two long tables, carried by the pointy heads and the meat heads. The midgets, including the one he had seen the day before in the porkpie, appeared, carrying bowls, pans, and silverware. The midgets had an attitude about them that made you think they might break down and start cussing and throwing things at any moment.

The stove was fired up by a fellow that looked to be made of coat hangers and a thin coating of flesh. When Skinny got the grease in the frying pan going, eggs were cracked by the meat heads and dumped into the pan and the pancake batter was whipped by the pointy heads and poured onto buttered griddles. The fat lady with the beard began to flip and cook the pancakes and took over the egg chores from the meat heads. Conrad made an appearance, rearing up on his hind legs to stand at the stove and talk to the fat lady.

Skinny found a camp stool and a pack of cigarettes and began to smoke and look off thoughtfully into the bright damp morning, as if everything he might ever need to do had just been done.

It all went like clockwork. Flipping pancakes, whipping eggs, pouring milk. Soon the table was set and Frost came out of his trailer. Everyone exchanged good mornings, then Frost saw Bill standing near the Ice Man's trailer and waved him over.

Frost slapped a spot on the plank table's seat, and Bill sat there and the fat lady with the beard put plates heaped with pancakes and eggs in front of them.

In time more people came out of trailers, and many of them appeared normal, just fat or tattooed or tired-looking.

Soon everyone but the pretty blonde, who had not shown herself this morning, was seated at the tables. A prayer was said by one of the meat heads that sounded as if he were gargling stew, then the eating began. Everything was mannerly and neat. Forks and napkins and pass this and thank you please. Neat except for Double Buckwheat, who

Bill now realized were retards. They banged heads and gnawed at the same pancake and were soon covered in syrup and had egg in their hair. Moments later, they were rolling in the dying grass slapping at each other as if attacking flies.

They grunted and cussed and called each other nigger this and nigger that, and kept rolling and slapping. They were ignored by the others, and in time the fighting stopped; the retards, now not only coated in syrup and eggs but covered in grass and dirt and stray ants, returned to the table and went about fighting over a fresh pancake and a glass of milk, which ended up spilled and flowing across the table.

Pretty soon the pair were tumbling across the grass again, cussing, grunting, and calling each other nigger.

The fat lady with the beard produced a towel and mopped up the milk, then wrung the towel out on the ground, coiled it, and popped it at the retards, hitting one in the throat.

"Settle down, now," she said, and they went at it more slowly for a while, but they didn't stop.

"One hurts the other," Bill asked Frost, "does it hurt both of them?"

"Yes," said Frost, eating a bite of pancake. "They are two but are one. They seem to like fighting. It's something they do. Every morning. Every meal. And sometimes between meals. You get used to it."

Bill thought: Not goddamn likely.

Twelve

Bill found the freaks distracting. The two rolling around on the ground, bathed in syrup and eggs and milk and grass, did nothing for his appetite either.

Frost grabbed Bill's arm and smiled at him. Bill was surprised to find that Frost had a powerful grip. He looked somewhat doughy, and the white hair, blue eyes, pale skin, and occasional flush of red on his face made him seem soft and weak, but he was actually quite strong. A beardless Santa on steroids.

Frost said, "The swelling on your face has gone down slightly."

Bill had forgotten about his face. It didn't hurt. It didn't even itch. Without thinking, he raised a hand to his face and felt the lumps and had a sudden fear they might not go away.

"Come with me," Frost said.

He and Frost walked away from the breakfast table toward the trailers. Frost said, "What I need, Bill, is someone to work for me."

"Looks like you got plenty of help here."

"I do, but the truth of the matter is, except for Conrad, who is my right-hand man, these people are quite busy with running their acts. Taking care of their trailers, the like."

"Then what would I do?"

"I need someone to help manage. To help organize. I do most of that myself. Conrad does the rest, but I need someone who can fit in with the general populace. Someone that isn't special in appearance."

"What about the blonde?"

"My wife, Gidget. I can't say she cares much for my day-to-day activities. I find her a blessing, but she can be distracting too. To put it bluntly, that isn't really any of your business."

"Sure," Bill said politely, smelling money behind all this, and wondering if the blonde was some kind of freak herself. Maybe had a cock and balls.

"What I can do is give you room and board and nothing else."

"Oh."

"I know that isn't very promising, but that's temporary. After a month or two we can evaluate how the two of us feel about one another, and we can decide if we'd like to continue together. If you like, next town, while your face is swollen like that, we can let you in on the freak show."

"As a freak?"

"While you look like one, yes. We'll come up with a name for you." Frost's face took on a disappointed look.

"When your face heals, I'm afraid there won't be much point in that. But—freaks get tips. Sometimes, they make pretty good. The Afro-American twins, Elvis and Thomas, are favorites. I think because they fight with one another . . . Wouldn't that be terrible? To not like one another and to be tied together forever."

"I know I wouldn't care for it."

"One believes he is lighter skinned than the other, and that is a source of friction between them."

"I thought they were just stupid."

"Retardation plays a part. But so does skin color. Actually, I believe the two of them are exactly the same shade."

"They both look like niggers to me. Actually, you think about it, they're just one two-headed nigger."

Frost stopped walking. "Bill, if you're going to work for me, and I know you haven't agreed to, you're going to have to have more respect for these people, and for other races. I can't tolerate that kind of talk. Retards. Niggers. This is all outside of my beliefs, and this is my train, as I like to refer to it. So, if this is my train, and I'm the engineer, and you want to ride on it, there are some rules. One. Do not denigrate my freaks. The word freak itself is acceptable. In fact, they call themselves freaks."

"I heard the retar—the black fellas calling each other nigger."

"There is that. But I hope you understand what I'm saying. I'd like to have you here, but if you're going to speak of my people that way, I'll have to ask you to leave."

Bill studied Frost's face. He looked stern and serious. Bill thought: Asshole. Freak lover. Freak yourself. Nigger lover. But he said, "I understand. I don't mean nothin' by what I say sometimes. I'll try to be more feeling."

"Good. Then you'll stay?"

"Sure," Bill said.

Thirteen

The train, as Frost called it, traveled out of there that day after breakfast with Frost driving a green Chevy station wagon with Gidget in it and all the others following. Frost left Bill to drive his motor home. Frost explained that he normally drove the home and Gidget the Chevy, but now that Bill was working for the freak show, he got to drive the motor home.

They arrived at a little town called Wellington Mills about midday. They parked the trucks and cars and trailers in a field just inside of town. Some of the trailers had sides that opened up and they opened them and propped them so that they might serve as counters for selling hot dogs and pretzels and all manner of junk. They put together little frames with curtains on them and set them about the field and stuffed them full of pins to knock down and hoops and buckets and jars to toss pennies or balls into, arranged stuffed animals all about, the cheap sort with eyes children could peel off and swallow.

They put up some large tents and a couple of fitted grandstands where you could sit, and they brought out and put together a few rides, the tiltawhirl being prominent, but the guy who owned and operated it called it a whirligig and so everyone else did. It was old and rusty with badly painted metal bucket seats. The paint was green, but time had taken a toll on it. When the wind blew, the bolts that held it together—and it was missing a few—rattled and the whirligig buckets swung slightly and the whole thing creaked and made you think of bodies with shards of metal poking through them. The guy who ran it looked like an ex-con and was. He was the second oiliest man in the carnival. Only a fellow worked there with two teeth was nastier looking. A guy called Potty, which was what was suspected of being under his fingernails.

Phil liked to mention he was an ex-con, but he was sketchy on the crime he had committed and how much time he had done. He wore a sleeveless white T-shirt with a cigarette cocked behind his ear. He had lots of tattoos, most of them done with a pocketknife and the residue from match heads. But he had some professional tattoos. Brightly colored devil heads. Women with oversized breasts and their legs spread. A trio of blood-dripping hearts with a sword through them. He had plenty of grease in his hair. You'd have thought that much grease had to be an accident. Like some mean oversized men had held him down and rubbed it in there and made him wear it.

Phil had interesting teeth and a lot of nose. He talked about sex a lot, who he'd done and who he wanted to do. Bill didn't know any of his list of previously screwed. Gidget was mentioned in the lineup of potential pokes. But so

were a number of models and movie starlets. Phil claimed
to be the best ride operator in the place, and considering
the only other rides were a merry-go-round with paint-
flaked horses and a kind of slanting bucket ride that didn't
go any faster than a fat man could run in heavy boots, Bill
didn't doubt this. Mostly the carnival wasn't about rides. It
was tossing hoops and throwing baseballs and looking at
weird shit and freaky people.

Phil was talkative, had a flask with some whiskey in it, and
wasn't too good to share. Bill figured this was partly because
he wanted to tell his stories to someone that hadn't heard
them and might not know any better.

They sat in one of the whirligig buckets for a while and
passed the flask back and forth. The flask was greasy where
Phil had been running his fingers through his hair.

"I been thinking about chuckin' this carnival shit in,"
Phil said.

"Yeah."

"Yeah. I mean, in your case, that head and all, you kind
of got to stick with it now that you're here, but me, I been
thinking about moving on."

Bill told him that his head was swollen from mosquito
bites.

"Say it is?"

"Yep."

"You're yankin' me?"

"Nope."

"No shit?"

"No shit."

"Well, I'll be goddamned. I never seen anything like
that. You look naturally fucked-up to me, but then again,
could be the light."

"I think I got some kind of allergic reaction."

"Yeah, I knowed of a guy got that way when he ate anything made out of wheat. 'Course he wasn't bad as you are. I'm like that with the clap."

Bill didn't have a lot of medical training, but he didn't think the clap was that kind of disease, and as far as he knew it didn't make your head swell, the big one anyway. Then again he had never had the clap, so he let it ride. Instead he focused on the wheat.

"Couldn't eat wheat, huh?"

"Pie. Cake. Bread. Anything with wheat flour in it, made his face like a pizza and he bloated up like something dead."

They sat and drank awhile, then Phil looked up at the whirligig buckets above them, said, "What I want to do is maybe start a little collection agency. You know, kind of buy up bad debts, then collect 'em."

"But what if you don't collect 'em?"

"You lose. But you can buy the debts for less than is owed if they've been owed awhile and the folks owed can't get their money. They're glad to get out from under 'em and sell 'em to you. Then it's up to you to get shed of 'em."

"How do you do that any better than they did?"

"You go see people. You try to get them to pay up on stuff. They don't, you got to strong-arm 'em a little. Threats are enough sometimes. You know, kind of push 'em around till they come up with the dough. I knowed of a nigger used to do that and he made pretty good jack doing it. He had a good car. You're a stout-looking fella. I bet you could do good with something like that, we went in together. We could beat the shit out of 'em if they didn't pay."

"I don't think so," Bill said.

"We wouldn't have to do it with our fists. We could get some blackjacks or sticks or something. Gotta tape them sticks though, or your hand'll slip. I got that on good authority from the nigger I was telling you about. He said you got a good heavy stick and hit someone with it, every damn time your hand would slip. He solved that with a little tape."

Bill thought: Shit, I can't even rob a firecracker stand, let alone beat money out of deadbeats. "I don't think so."

"Well, you might be right. I figure running a little ring of whores might be easier. It's mostly them that get arrested. You're the pimp, you just get the gravy. And you get free pussy too. Now think about that."

"Reckon that's true," Bill said.

"Think about it. Could be a career move. You and me could shake this place and go into business right away."

"It's something, I guess. But I don't know."

"Just think about it."

"I will."

"When I was sixteen I fell off a brick truck."

"Yeah."

"Hit my head. It did something to my dick."

"Beg pardon."

"Something in your brain controls your dick. I mean what makes it stand up and all. Nerves, muscles, all that. It's connected to the brain. It made me semihard all the time. I mean, I want to do it, you know, it gets harder, but I've got a permanent partial hard-on right this minute."

Bill refrained from glancing at Phil's crotch, for fear the gentleman might produce his tool as evidence. Bill didn't want to open any doors there.

"It's got benefits. I strip off the skivvies, gal sees the ole hammer and it ain't even hard and she's looking at six

71

inches, well, it starts you off right, you know. There are problems, pants never fit right. Always feel a little tucked in, you know."

Phil moved from dicks to politics. He seemed to be against a lot of things and not for anything much. Bill zoned him out and nodded from time to time and took his turn at the whiskey.

The flask got finished off about the time Phil finished up a story about his days as a gigolo. Bill thanked Phil, got out of the whirligig bucket, and wandered around until he was commandeered for work again.

Bill thought this whole gig sucked, and being half drunk didn't help either. Bill had to be told several times what to do. He was mostly told by the bearded lady who everyone called U.S. Grant, because her beard and stout appearance put one in mind of the Civil War hero and former president. She was grumpy and bossy and partial to colorful knee-length shifts that only had to have a hole for the head and arms. She had enough hair on her stout legs to make one of those Russian hats. Bill sort of wished he'd stayed in the bucket and talked whores, beating people up for money, half-hard dicks, and politics with Phil, even if all the whiskey was gone.

While the carnival was being set up, Frost drove the Chevy into town for something or another. Gidget didn't go with him. She hung out in the motor home. Bill thought about her in there, and wondered if she might be naked, about to take a bath. Thinking like that helped him get through his work.

When Bill finished working, he walked over to Conrad, who sat on his ass like a dog by the Ice Man's trailer. Conrad was shaking a cigarette out of a pack and lighting a smoke, looking at the painting on the side of the trailer. He sucked smoke in and blew it out his doggie nose and put his cigarettes and lighter away.

Conrad spoke to Bill without turning to look at him, a greeting, but it kind of shook Bill. The guy not only looked like a dog, he had hearing like one too.

"Cigarette?" Conrad asked, and turned away from the painted figure on the trailer and looked at Bill.

Bill shook his head and asked Conrad how things worked in this business. It was something to say.

"Mr. Frost goes into town and spreads flyers around. We already have the permits for here and every place we're going. He gets them in advance. We have a regular line of little towns we make across Texas, some in Louisiana."

Bill tried not to watch Conrad talk. It was too weird watching a dog's lips move and words come out. Especially a dog with a mustache and a cigarette dangling from his mouth.

"He'll also have to pay some kickbacks so we can stay parked here, 'cause you see, in lots of places showing freaks is against the law. 'Course we do it anyway 'cause people want to see it and pay to see it. We'll get things ready here, tonight we'll do our job, which is mostly sitting around, yelling a few things at the crowd."

"How's that?"

"Folks like a few things said, but you got to not go too far. If you do, you could get in trouble. Way we look, you can only push so far, then people want to hurt you. They think it's okay to hurt you if you look different, 'cause they don't think you're human like them."

Bill thought: Correctamundo.

"They like me to bark and be a little scary so they can feel better than me, like I ain't the kind of guy wants the same things they do, but you can push it too much. I've seen it happen. The coloreds, they get it the worst. Even though they aren't that bright, they know when to shut up. They don't, some of these goobers might take two ropes to them and string 'em up."

Bill tried to envision that. A Siamese twin hanging.

"How'd Frost come by all these people?"

"They're more of us than some folks think. You ought to know that. Frost is like flypaper. Freaks find and stick to him. Or the people who manage the freaks, like the parents of the two-headed colored, they sell 'em to Frost. Most of 'em are better off actually. Frost treats people good. He's done you all right, hasn't he?"

"Reckon he has."

"Then we got folks here that are scams."

"Scams?"

"They ain't real freaks. They just doctor themselves up. Have you seen our half and half?"

Bill shook his head.

"She's around. Kind of snooty. Sticks to herself. Shaves one side of her head, does a bit of makeup to give a beard to one cheek and jaw, talks out of the side of her mouth on that side like a man. On the other side she has long hair, no whiskers, and talks like a woman. She's a woman though."

"She got tits on both sides, don't she?"

"Yeah, but she ain't got big ones, so she pads the one on the woman side and wraps the other one down. Even wears a sock stuffed with more socks in her pants, on her right side, like she's hangin', you know. Claims she's got both the hammer and the split. There's real folks got both kinds of equipment, you know, but they ain't split down the middle, and she ain't one of them. There's some others like that here; scams, I mean. Claiming they're one thing or another but they ain't none of it. And there's the Pickled Punks. It's the trailer ain't open yet. The long one."

"Pickled Punks?"

"You'll see them tonight. Babies died at birth, or early on. Ones with tails and too many legs, heads, eyeballs, or what have you. Babies had they lived would have grown up to look like some of us. They're in jars of preservative— pickled, you see. Folks like to look at them."

"What about the Ice Man?"

Conrad the Wonder Dog was silent for a moment. "That's special."

"Is it a fake?"

"Frost came by it years ago, you see. It don't sound like much, but once you see it . . . Well, there ain't nothing like it. It's special. I don't look at it anymore. Damn thing bothers me."

Bill thought: You ain't got no mirrors in your trailer.

"Is it fake?" he asked again.

"All these paintings on the sides of trailers, they make all of us more than we are. You should see my trailer. Way it's painted, I look exactly like a dog with some human features."

Yes, thought Bill, and . . .

"But you look at us, you don't see what you see on the side of the trailer. Same with the others. The paintings make us something we aren't. They work on the mind. The Ice Man, his painting, it ain't nothing to what's inside. They can't paint what's inside, and they can't make it any more than what it is, and yet, it ain't nothing but this body layin' there in a freezer. It's nothing much and everything there is."

"Is it fake?"

"It is what it is," Conrad said.

Bill didn't quite get what Conrad was saying, but he didn't know how to ask him to explain himself. Conrad had finished his cigarette and had returned his attention to the painting of the Ice Man.

"For someone with a big head, you talk all right. I thought maybe you'd be short on brains. A lot of big heads, they're like that. More water than gray matter. Not that it's their fault."

"I ain't normally this way. I was mosquito-bit."

"What?"

Bill told him again, this time with some explanation, but he left the firecracker stand and the dead deputy out of it. In other words, everything he told Conrad, except for being lost in the swamp and being mosquito-bit, was a downright lie.

Conrad nodded his head, said, "Oh, you're like one of the scams" and went away, as if Bill's company embarrassed him.

Bill was kind of disappointed he hadn't turned the conversation to sex. He wanted to know if the dog was getting any, and if he had to do it doggie style. Now it was too late, Conrad was gone. Another mystery was left unanswered.

Bill thought he might like to go back to Frost's trailer and hang out, but the blonde, Gidget, was still in there, and he was ashamed of how he looked and he didn't want to be brutalized further by her ambivalence.

Glancing in the direction of the trailer, he saw her come out. She had on those great shorts and they were way unzipped, held up only by her hips. Another inch down and he would have been able to see the hole show. She was wearing flip-flops and a very tight white T-shirt that was rough cut along the midriff. Her unbridled titties bobbed under the material and poked their .45 caliber tips at the fabric. She came down the steps and trod lightly along and glided past some trailers, on across the field, down a slight rise, and out of sight.

Bill wandered that way until he could see her again. She was sitting down on a lump of dirt smoking a cigarette, looking across the field, through a barbed wire fence, at a bunch of trees and some cows milling about.

He decided right then wasn't any way she had a dick. She was all woman. Bill thought about trying to make small talk, but the way he looked he didn't want to do it. He walked back into the camp and waited for nightfall and thought about how things might be going with the law.

He wondered if they were on to him or if he could go home. He wondered how his Mama was doing in the bedroom. If any more of her had melted down and if some kind of bugs had gotten into the house and were crawling all over her.

He got home, and everything was all right, first thing he had to do was get rid of Mama. Maybe drag her out back on that mattress and set her on fire or something. Pick up what was left with a yard rake, bag it, and send it to the dump.

Shit, Bill thought. I can't do anything right. Can't even do a simple robbery without it going bad. That goddamn string on the mask breaking, the flat tire, the deputy, Fat Boy and Chaplin biting the big one. And Mama dying and having the kind of handwriting she did and me not being able to copy it. There is the source of my entire problem. Her stinginess and her bad handwriting.

Way things were going, he was going to end up in jail,

or if that didn't happen and he got away with things, then he might have to get a job.

The thought of that made him weak in the knees. This damn freak show was work enough and already he didn't like it, but it beat the alternatives.

Whatever they were.

Fourteen

The night arrived and Frost came back. He called out this and he called out that. He pointed and nodded, shook his head and stood with hands on his hips. Things began to happen.

Trailers and cars were pulled in a tight circle. Battery trailers powered up the lights and made them bright. The lights were white and yellow, red and blue, a tossing of green and gold. The whirligig in the glow of the lights became fresh and new, an alien craft waiting to take on passengers.

The crude paintings on the sides of the trailers changed as well. They became sexual, alluring. There was cheap carnival music playing, and barkers, or talkers as they called themselves, stood in front of tents and trailers and called out as cars parked and people entered the carnival through the gap in the wall of trailers where the tickets were sold.

Bill didn't have his own place as a freak, as Frost had suggested, and he didn't want one. The idea disgusted him. He was ashamed enough to walk about with his face messed up the way it was, so he pushed himself back into the shadows by the Ice Man's trailer and waited there and watched.

It was strange to see what the trailers and tents had become. How it all seemed so fine and rare. Children laughed and ate cotton candy from the stands, and young women in short-shorts and tight-fitting shirts walked about and laughed and seemed impressed and amused by everything. Boys with acne and greasy hair poked each other with elbows, looked at girls and grinned, then laughed one to the other.

The freak tents and trailers were busy, but the Ice Man's business was slow. However, as people came and left the Ice Man's trailer, the word spread, and the same people who had been came back, and new ones came, and as the night went on the line grew and stayed long.

Two middle-aged policemen, one slim and one fat, came strolling through. On duty, probably, sent to see that all was well and the freaks weren't planning a hostile takeover of the town. The cops seemed to be enjoying the women in shorts as much as the acne-faced boys. They had the same grins and elbow motions.

From time to time men and women stopped and watched Bill in the shadows, his face looking all the more strange there, holding darkness behind knots and grooves of mosquito injury. But no one spoke to him, until the cops.

One of the cops, the slim one, saw him in the shadows and said, "What're you supposed to be?"

Bill wondered if his photograph was on bulletins. He

wondered if his face could be recognized beneath the mosquito bites. He stepped out of the shadows, into the light.

"I'm the Blowed Up Man," he said.

"What?" said the skinny cop.

"The Blowed Up Man. My face blowed up."

The thin cop laughed. "Well, that ain't any kind of name. You need to come up with something better for a name."

"Yeah," said the fat cop. "That sucks. You could call yourself Mr. Ugly or Knot Head or something like that. That'd work better . . . You fucked up like that at birth?"

"Industrial accident."

"What kind of industrial accident?"

"Chicken plant blowed up and I was in it."

"What the hell blows up in a chicken plant?"

"Chickens."

The slim cop studied on that, then burst out laughing. "You're pulling my leg, ain't you?"

"I was hit in the face by flyin' chickens. They ate too much and one of 'em farted, and there was a foreman lighting a cigarette, and the rest of it's history. It's called the Great Owentown Chicken Disaster. Look it up, it's in the records."

"Now I know you're pullin' my leg," said the slim cop, and he laughed some more, just like this was the best thing he'd ever heard.

"Come on now," said the fat cop. "It wasn't at birth, how'd it happen?"

"A fire."

"Well, you look it," said the fat cop. "I got a question. It's somethin' I'd like to know. Somethin' I've always wondered about people like you."

"All right."

"A face like that, you get much pussy?"

Bill found himself irritated by this, but realized it was the same question he had asked Frost about Conrad.

"I do all right."

"You get any good pussy—I mean, anyone ain't messed up or got a disease? I can see you gettin' the bearded lady, or the one says she's got a dick and a hole, 'cause, I mean, what are their prospects? But what about good pussy?"

The cops looked up as Gidget appeared, butting her way through the crowd, her face sullen, her lips puffed out as if they had just been punched. She had on her open front shorts and the same tight top. A couple of boys stood nearby in all their pus-pocked grandeur, watching Gidget float by, showing her all the openmouthed reverence of two monks approaching a religious shrine.

"Like that?" said the fat cop.

"Not that," Bill said. "Not yet anyway."

The cops laughed. The fat one said, "Yeah, right, brother, not yet. Somethin' like that, and somethin' like you, well, you ain't even got money she'd want if she was sellin' it."

"A fire, huh?" said the skinny one.

Bill nodded.

"Yeah," said the skinny one. "I can see that, like your face caught on fire and someone put it out with a back hoe."

Both cops laughed.

"One thing's for sure," said the fat one, "whatever happened it happened bad, and you are one ugly dude. Come to think of it, I don't know that bearded woman would want you after all."

"Well, now," the skinny one said, "you have a good night, Blowed Up Man or Burned Up Man, or Chicken

Hit Man, whatever you are, and don't bring that face into town. You might make a pregnant nigger woman throw a child, you hear?"

The cops laughed themselves away from him and pushed ahead in the line to the Ice Man's trailer. When they came out of the trailer a few minutes later they were quiet.

They walked on through the carnival and out of sight behind the whirligig, probably on their way to demanding free hot dogs and drinks and cotton candy, ready to peek at adolescent girl asses bending over counters as the girls tossed coins or baseballs.

Bill said softly: "Dumb shits."

Fifteen

Bill passed the Ice Man's trailer and went in the direction Gidget had gone. She had slipped through the circle of trailers and was at her earlier spot, sitting on the ground smoking a cigarette in the dark. Her gold hair held the moonlight and it fell butter smooth over her skin, delighted to be there. The white smoke from her cigarette was rising up into the night and floating over her like a venomous cloud. Somewhere off in the distant dark a cow bellowed sadly, as if it had just figured out its true purpose in life.

Bill walked up behind Gidget. "Nice night, huh."

She didn't turn to look at him. "Get lost, shithead. You ain't gettin' nothin'."

"I'm just being friendly."

"Howdy. Now fuck off, pencil dick."

"You ain't very nice."

"No, I ain't, and there ain't no reason for you to be out here hustlin' my ass. I don't fuck freaks. Let me smoke my cigarette. It's about all the fun I get."

"I just want to talk."

"Sure you do. Now fuck off, or I'll tell Frost you were bothering me."

"You're his woman, I wouldn't try to hustle you none."

"Bad enough I got to be in this freak show. I don't want to buddy up to a pomegranate head. Screw off. Now!"

Bill turned and trudged back through the gap in the trailers, throwing up little heaps of pasture as he went. He thought: Hell, I ain't no pomegranate head. I'm just bug-bit and allergic. Ain't Frost told her that?

For want of anything better to do, and to help nurse his trampled feelings, he went over to the Ice Man's trailer and got in line. Conrad, on break, came strolling by on all fours. He saw Bill in line.

"You ain't got to stand in line you want to see somethin'," Conrad said. "Go on in. You're privileged."

"Hey, Fido," said a guy in line dressed in a red and white barber pole jacket and rust-colored slacks. He had less grease on his hair than Phil, but he certainly had enough up there to do him and still deep-fry a chicken. "Everyone ought to wait in line, even pimple head here."

"He works for the carnival," Conrad said.

"It's all right," Bill said. "I don't mind waitin'."

"You don't have to wait," Conrad said.

"I say he does," said Barber Pole.

"Say what you want," Conrad said.

Barber Pole mentally flipped over a series of insults and finally arrived at: "Hey, Fido. You do it doggie style?"

A man standing with Barber Pole, a jar-headed redneck with a tavern tumor and white shoes that were brand-new about 1968, snickered. "A face like that, he don't do it any kinda style."

Conrad, accustomed to insults, sat back on his haunches and fished for a cigarette. He gave Barber Pole and his pal a contemptuous look, like a cantankerous dog who won't do a trick in front of his master's friends. "Who the fuck dresses you, Ronald McDonald?" Conrad put the smoke between his lips. "I had a coat like that, I'd shit on it before I wore it." He lit the cigarette. "It'd make it look about three times better."

"Why you freaky piece of trash," said Barber Pole, moving toward Conrad.

Conrad held up one leather-wrapped hand. "You're gonna lose your place in line, you step out. And worse, you might get your funky redneck ass whipped."

Now everyone in the Ice Man line glanced apprehensively at Conrad and Barber Pole, tried to appear as if they weren't really looking. Curious, but not wanting to be sucked into things.

"I ought to kick you," said Barber Pole, but he hadn't come any nearer.

Conrad plucked the cigarette from his mouth and flicked it away. "What you ought to do is get you a decent haircut and a better run of clothes from the Goodwill and maybe scrape a layer off your teeth and drain your hairdo, is what you ought to do. And if you folded some paper or cardboard thick enough in them shoes, they might give you a half inch of needed height."

The man came out of the line then, and Conrad, not really making any effort about it, reached into his red overalls and produced a razor and flicked it open with his left hand and brought out another pack of cigarettes with his right and used the razor to slice the top. He used his rubbery lips to pull a smoke from the pack and he put the pack away and continued to hold the open razor. He got his lighter with his free hand and flicked it and put the flame to the cigarette. He looked at Barber Pole out of the corner of his eye and put the lighter away, said, "You do what you're thinkin', I'm gonna do what you think I'm thinking."

Barber Pole turned to look at his companion, who appeared to be no longer interested. He was in line, staring straight ahead. You would have thought he'd have never been aware of anything but the Ice Man. He craned his neck forward as if he were examining the movement of the line, maybe hoping to see the Ice Man make an appearance at the doorway of the trailer.

Barber Pole huffed and puffed a bit, and after a moment he left the line and wandered off. "I'm gonna talk to the cops about you."

"Give 'em my best wishes," Conrad said.

Conrad put the razor away, blew smoke, said to Bill, "Go on in."

"Ain't you goin'?"

"No. I think about it now and then, but I don't go see it anymore."

Bill broke line and pushed past an old couple in the doorway who started at his appearance. The old woman grabbed the old man and nearly knocked him off the steps, sent his Panama hat flying. A boy of twelve in a Cub Scout suit leaned out of line and picked up the hat and took off his scout cap and put the Panama on his head and said, "Look, I'm a bird feeder."

The old man snatched the hat off the Cub Scout's head and put it on and glared at the twelve-year-old, who didn't seem intimidated in the least. He had an air about him that said, I've taken better beatin's than you can give. The little Cub Scout put on his hat and cocked it at a rakish angle and stared the old man down, then looked at the old woman as if he might ask her for a date and make her buy the rubbers.

Bill slipped inside. It was very cool in there. Goose bumps broke out on his arms and the backs of his hands. Frost was dressed in a white suit with pale blue shoes and a pale blue shirt and dark blue tie. His socks were thin and his pants were short and you could see the socks were held up with black silk garters. He was sitting in a chair on a raised platform at the back of the trailer and he had his feet cocked back and hung behind one of the chair rungs, which was what allowed his pants to hike up and his socks and garters to be seen. He was bathed in a bright light from a bare overhead bulb. It gave him a kind of glow, like a skid row angel. In front of him was a deep freezer and over the freezer where a lid should have been was a glass plate beaded up like a cold beer mug. Frost had a hair dryer plugged in and lying in his lap, and when there were enough people to surround the freezer, he turned on the hair dryer and waved it over the glass a bit. The cloud on the glass faded and people looked down and changed their expressions. They craned their necks and turned their heads and leaned forward and tilted back and looked at what was in the freezer from all angles. One man, holding his little boy in his arms, said, "My almighty."

The little boy, possibly four years old, leaned forward for a look and said, "Daddy, don't he get cold?"

The man laughed, said, "Reckon he don't get much of anything."

"Let me tell you about him," Frost said suddenly over the roar of the dryer. He cut the device and leaned back in his chair. He had already given this spiel a hundred times tonight, but now his face looked as fresh as a young woman's tittie. Now that Frost was about to tell his story, something about his body changed. He still slumped in his chair, but it was as if he were a jack-in-the-box and someone had pressed a heavy weight on his head to keep him from springing up.

He lowered his eyes to the glass plate over the freezer, which was once again clouded with cold. Frost's beautiful blue eyes were soft as a summer cloud.

"There are all manner of stories about our man here. He came to me like this from another carnival. All that was left of the carnival was this and a display of giant Russian rats. The old man running the carnival only showed his exhibits at tractor pulls and the like and he was tired and wanting to retire. He couldn't feed the rats or afford the electricity to keep the body in shape and he didn't like the tractor pulls because the noise hurt his ears. His last tractor pull, the heavyweight champion of the world and a group that sang gospel songs were supposed to show, but the boxer canceled and one of the gospel singers died in route, so the show lost its entertainment, except for the Ice Man and the rats. The Ice Man was displayed poorly, in near darkness, and when people saw the rats there was darn near a riot. Disappointed, ready to quit anyway, the owner gave me an opportunity and I took it.

"I was forced to buy rats and body, all in one swoop. The rats are no longer with us. They broke loose and are probably in the East Texas bottoms going under the guise of possums now."

A little laugh from the crowd. Nothing to warm your heart, but a chuckle. One man said softly to the woman he was with, "Iff'n niggers ain't killed and ate 'em."

Frost gave this man a stare and the man cleared his throat, turned his attention to what was in the freezer, but he held a smile on his face, like a child who had farted softly in church and was proud of it. The woman he was with, dressed in a faded green pants suit and uncomfortable shoes, wilted slightly and smiled at Frost as if to let him know she wasn't that way and felt sorry for her companion's ignorance, but what could you do.

Bill tried to get a look at the exhibit. He strained his neck and his eyes, but all he could see was the frosty glass top and something shadowy beneath. There was a bit of room around the freezer, and he could have slid in there for a look, but he kept himself pulled back and out of the way. He didn't want to draw any more attention to himself than he had to. Already a few people were taking sly looks at him.

"The history of this body is more complex. I bought it from the carnival, but the owner of the carnival bought it from a man who claimed it was a wild man shot up in Wisconsin. It hasn't been shot, however. The wounds you see are from something else. Another story is this body was found in an ice floe and that it is the body of a Neanderthal trapped in a glacier during a prehistoric storm. If that is the case, there is no telling how old it is. Perhaps someday I will have it carbon-dated, but as you can tell from looking at it, it is unique and ancient, yet fresh and new as tomorrow. This is the story I believe, the one about the ice, and he is still in ice, figuratively anyway, and here in front of you is a man from across the centuries, a forerunner to who we are now."

"Yeah, or he's just some fella died and got put in a freezer," said the man who had remarked about the possums.

The woman with him, as if to stay in Frost's good graces, said, "You can tell he ain't no regular man."

"Might be Big Foot," the man with her said. "And talkin' about feet, he's got something between his toes too. Dog poo maybe."

The woman took the man by the arm and hustled him out with the others, and in between the next group, Bill eased forward and took a peek.

At first he saw nothing other than finger writing on the frosty glass where someone, the talkative man perhaps, had written *Alley Oop*.

Then Frost turned on the hair dryer and let it blow across the top of the glass, warming it. The condensation peeled away and the writing retreated. Bill was startled at what he could see. He was clearly looking at a man, but it was not a withered tar-colored husk as he had expected. Here was a naked man near six feet tall with pink skin and very clear features. He had a large forehead and wide jaws, a long slightly crooked nose and lips like fat fishing worms. There were little wounds on his forehead, and another beneath the short ribs on the left side. He had a thick black beard and a full head of hair and the hair was thick on his shoulders, chest, groin, and legs. The eyes were wide open and blue without pupils, slicked over by the cold, but those eyes, so blue, so strange, seemed to see right up and through the glass into Bill's head. Those eyes made him think about things, all manner of things, and all at once.

The glass filmed over again, and Frost waved the dryer over the lid once more, chasing the icy curtain away. This time Bill took note of the corpse's short, yellow teeth, touched by a gloss of refrigerated winter and the bright light, giving them the appearance of being carved from dirty soap and greased with Vaseline. He looked at the rough hands and feet, the man's penis and testicles. He was pleased to discover the man's sexual apparatus was not as large as his own; it was neither an acorn nor a hose, but in shape and size like peckers and nuts on white marble statues made by the ancients, uncircumcised and covered by a flap of skin like a pantyhose pulled over a face, huddled silent in a patch of wiry black hair, a masked creature bent on filling station robbery that had died in its nest.

Bill and Frost exchanged glances, and a slow smile came over Frost's lips and Bill turned and went out alongside the line which was now three times as long as before and still growing. He did not see Conrad. He didn't see anyone he knew from the carnival. He went out and through the gap in the trailers and walked across the pasture to where Gidget had been. She was gone now, and he was glad, because something inside of him was all turned around, and he thought if she were there he might hit her. He felt as he had felt when his mother died and he realized no more checks were forthcoming. He felt as if he had awakened for the first time only to discover that permanent sleep was better.

He sat where Gidget had sat, and the spot was damp with her, and warm, and the night was warm and the sky was clear. Way off in the distance he heard the cow moo again, long and harsh, like a plea for help, and he wished to hell it would die and everyone else would die and just leave him alone in the pasture, in the warm night, under the clear sky, and then he would fade and fade until he was nothing but a dot in the dark, then not even that.

PART THREE

Gidget

Sixteen

Bill's days and nights rolled one into another, same into same, driving from town to town, helping set the carnival up, then hanging out until it was time to do it all over again.

He hated it. Work had never agreed with him, but at his most down-and-out moment he had never considered working with a dog-man, a bearded lady, assorted ruined heads, damaged bodies, and a pleasant man with a hand growing out of his tit. He had never thought of himself as way up on the food chain, but had felt he was above such as this, and now he was more than slightly troubled to discover he was wrong.

Mama was right again. He was not only stupid, he was a loser. Everywhere he turned he was socked with the mallet of stupidity, kicked in the balls by fate, given a dunce hat and the finger.

He considered leaving, then he'd run his hand over his face and dismiss the idea. Where would he go? He was a freak himself. He no longer found himself able to look in the mirror and had finally quit touching his face, even when it itched, and it had really begun to itch.

Sometimes at night when the carnival was in swing, he loitered outside the Ice Man's trailer, like a boy whose former lover was dating someone else, so he parks his car near her house, watching, mooning, not knowing what to do. He had not been back in to see the Ice Man, but the image of those eyes was burned into the back of his head as deep as a radiation wound.

Sometimes when he lay down at night he felt as if the Ice Man's eyes were falling out of the blackness toward him, then he would feel it was he who was falling. Diving down toward those two dark pools, then, just before he was drowned by them, he would wake up.

When he wasn't thinking about that, he was thinking about Gidget and about what was behind the zipper of those shorts she wore. He thought about that more than the Ice Man, especially every night at bedtime.

He had been moved out of Frost's bed and into the kitchen where Frost and Gidget had been sleeping. Now he could really hear their bed squeak at night, lots of grunts and groans. He thought old guys weren't supposed to get it up as much, but Frost was certainly doing something in there with Gidget, and he doubted he was teaching her wrestling holds.

When he was not asleep he thought less about Gidget and less about the Ice Man. Then he would lie awake on his cot and think about his mother, the house, his dead friends, and the cop in the creek. He wondered if Officer Cocksucker had been discovered yet. He wondered if the car he and his friends had stolen had been found at the bottom of the swamp, and if Fat Boy's car had been located.

Most likely. Skid marks would trace the car's demise as sure as railroad tracks would show the direction a train would take, and Fat Boy's own car would eventually be stumbled upon. He wondered if he had left some kind of DNA in the cars that would lead the cops to him. Sonofabitches were always finding DNA somewhere. Spit on your gum. Cum or shit stains in your shorts. Boogers in Kleenex.

That DNA crap always hung you unless you were a famous nigger football player.

One morning Frost knocked on the kitchen door and slid it back and came in carrying a flat black bag with a zipper. He sat on the bed next to Bill and said, "I got this for you."

Bill sat up and watched Frost unzip the bag. Inside were some pill bottles and some little bottles with liquid in them and two hypodermic needles.

"Hey," Bill said. "I don't do that shit."

"No, no," Frost said. "This isn't drugs. Well, it isn't illegal drugs. It's medicine."

"I didn't know I was sick."

Frost laughed. "You're infected with mosquito bites, my boy. I have a friend who supplied me with this stuff. A doctor. Did I tell you I was an RN for a time?"

Bill shook his head.

Frost took out one of the bottles and unscrewed the lid. Underneath there was a soft rubber cap stretched over the top of the bottle. Frost took one of the hypos and stuck the needle right through the rubber cap and drew some of the liquid into the hypo.

"I was lots of things before I was an owner of this carnival. But this is the only place I've ever really felt at home. With this hand on my chest I've always felt like an impostor to the outside world. This should help clear up some of the swelling, the low-grade infection. I have a couple of pills here I want you to take. We'd have done this sooner, my boy, but the truth be told, I had to wait until I came to the town where I had a doctor friend I used to know. He helped me out. I guess that does make them illegal drugs, doesn't it?"

Bill presented his arm to Frost, but Frost said, "No, has to be in the hip."

Reluctantly, Bill pulled down his underwear and rolled over and lay on his stomach, halfway expecting Frost's hands to clamp down on his shoulders and for Frost to enter him from behind. He had never known anyone like Frost, and no one had ever been as nice to him. Therefore, it occurred to Bill that Frost might be queer, looking for brown ring and deep penetration. Then it occurred to him if he was queer he was certainly banging one hell of a nice poontang about ten times a night. Did queers do that? Could they learn a trade like that and maybe even enjoy it?

The shot was over before Bill could consider much else, and Frost had not tried to impose himself. He merely cleaned his equipment with a little bottle of alcohol and put the hypo and the medicine away and zipped it up in the bag.

"I know you've done something you shouldn't, Bill," Frost said, "and I'm not asking what. I can read a man. I know men. I don't know women, but I know men. And you've done something. I know too you're a good man and it wasn't anything bad, just something stupid. Am I right?"

Bill hiked up his underwear and rolled over. "Yeah, I did some stuff. I told you already I did."

"All I want to know is what you've done isn't anything terrible. Just stupid. And you know better now."

"Yeah, I did plenty of stupid things. Stupid is kinda my trademark."

"Nothing like murder?"

Bill considered. He hadn't murdered his mother, she had died, and he hadn't murdered the idiot firecracker stand man, Chaplin had, and he hadn't killed Fat Boy, Fat Boy had gotten his from snakes, and he hadn't killed Chaplin, a Roman candle had, and he hadn't killed the cop. The cop managed that all by himself. For a man that hadn't killed anyone, he had certainly been around a lot of death, but he didn't even feel close to lying when he said: "Naw, nothing like murder. Just a little trouble. I reckon it'll blow over afore long. And yeah, I know better."

"Good," Frost said. "I've been watching you, and I think you're the man to do what I first asked you about."

"Managing?"

"Sort of. I need a man who can go into town and do some of the things I'm doing. I'm sick of it. I'll make a lot of the arrangements still, but I need someone to go in and pay some money here and there and pick up a few things and make sure permits are in order and advertising is taken care of. Got me?"

"I don't know anything about permits and that kind of stuff."

"Frankly, you don't have to. It's all arranged. Look, Bill, it isn't really a managing job. It's just donkey work, but it isn't difficult donkey work and I'd rather not do it. It's a way for you to start picking up a little money, and being a little more useful around here. Some of the others are starting to think you're some kind of pet of mine because you don't have oddities."

"Reckon I look odd enough."

"Everyone knows now it isn't a permanent oddity, and that you aren't trying to work up an oddity. I got to tell you straight, Bill, you have to do this, you want to stay on. We don't really need anyone else to just set things up."

"Am I gonna have to keep doing that too?"

"Yes. I said we don't need you, but you're here, you help."

"But this town stuff . . . With this face?"

"Another week, you'll be good as new."

"Yeah?"

"A little puffy, maybe, but lots better. Surely you've noticed it's better."

Bill, who had avoided examining his face for some time, went into the bathroom. Normally he just glanced into the sink and ran the water and washed his face and hands without looking in the mirror, but now he raised his head slowly and saw his reflection.

The Blowed Up Man was gone. He was puffy and red, even blue in a couple of spots. Knotty over the eyes, on the cheeks, at the corners of his lips, and right under the nose. Not pretty, but no one would mistake him for a freak now, just a guy who couldn't keep his hands up in a barroom brawl.

Bill washed and toweled his face dry, happy about the improvement. He came back in and sat down on the bed. "You're right, I'm gettin' better."

"These shots will make it cure up all the faster."

"This job going to actually pay me something besides room and board, huh?"

"That's what I said."

"How much?"

"It depends what we haul in. I take the money for entrance and for looking at the Ice Man, everyone else runs their own show. They take what they get for people looking at them, any tips they can finagle. I get a little slice of their pie so they can stay in the carnival. Way I'd do you is give you a percentage of what I get, plus room and board. You'll be in another trailer."

"What trailer?"

"The Ice Man's trailer. It's the only one with enough extra space. It's got facilities. I've even bought you some clothes. A few pairs of pants and T-shirts. A light jacket. Tennis shoes, socks, and underwear."

"Thanks."

"Don't mention it."

Feeling better, Bill became a shrewd businessman. He pursed his lips and narrowed his eyes. "I still don't know what kind of money we're talkin'."

"You'll find when I have a really good week I'll be generous. We usually do all right."

"Yeah, I'm surprised the jack this racket brings in. I always thought carnivals were by the skin of their teeth."

"It might seem like a lot to you, but by the time I deal with expenses and such it's no great shakes. The Ice Man, believe it or not, draws more people than anything."

"I've noticed."

"It's a full third of my income. There may come a time when I semiretire, and just put the Ice Man up somewhere for exhibit. I wouldn't have the expenses I have now, and it'd be a good living, I think. You see, people are getting so they don't like to look at freaks. Political correctness, I guess, but my children, the ones everyone else calls the Pickled Punks, and the Ice Man, people don't feel guilty

101

because they're already dead. They'll pay to look, because what they're looking at can't look back."

"That Ice Man, he what you said he was, a Neanderthal?"

"I said he might be. He looks a little too good to be a Neanderthal, don't you think?"

Bill wasn't really sure what a Neanderthal looked like, so he held back judgment. "You ever had the electricity go off on that thing? I mean, it did, wouldn't the Ice Man come to pieces pretty quick?"

"I'm prepared. What do you say? Is it a deal?"

They shook hands on it.

Seventeen

Bill awoke mornings atwist in his blankets, his cot squeaking as he rolled over and looked at the Ice Man's refrigerated tomb.

It was the same each day. He found living in the trailer with the Ice Man bothersome. At night, so he could sleep, he lay a blanket over the top of the freezer glass. He was uncertain what this accomplished, but it made him feel better.

Sometimes in a deep sleep he dreamed the Ice Man was breathing and he could hear it as certain as he could hear his own breath. In and out. And beyond the breathing was the thumping of a heart.

Thump. Thump. Thump. Most certainly the beating of an ancient bloodless heart. And there was the tapping at the glass. The tapping would grow more desperate, work in rhythm to the breathing and the pounding of the dead heart, and he would try to awake to make the dream end, but he feared if he awoke it would all be real. At least in the dream, he could call it a dream.

Other times he thought he heard the glass splintering, or thought he heard footsteps gliding up behind him, but when he broke the spell of sleep, turned with a start and an explosion of breath, there was only the freezer with the blanket stretched over it, its motor humming, and the beating of the little fan stirring hot air. He knew then the noise was the freezer and the fan and the outside wind rocking the trailer, working in tandem to scare the shit out of him.

If he turned the fan off, it grew hot and sticky and he couldn't sleep at all. So he ran the fan and it and the wind and the humming freezer gave him the Ice Man to deal with.

Except for bedtime the trailer wasn't so bad. During the day he drove Frost's motor home. The Ice Man's trailer was pulled by a semi-cab driven by Conrad. Conrad wore a black cowboy hat pulled low on his head. He was mounted on a leather cushion. He used a crutchlike device fastened to his leg to work the pedals. When he drove he assumed the appearance of a fella waiting for his last meal to pass.

When the caravan stopped it was soon show time. After the last customer left, the trailer was his again. He enjoyed it then, before there was the sound of the wind, the fan, and the freezer. He was even brave enough to place his dinner on the freezer glass and eat while looking at the Ice Man's face, clearing the glass from time to time with the hair dryer. Later, if they were near where he could pick up a channel, he would grapple with his aluminum-foil-covered rabbit ears, trying to bring in a TV station, or he would listen to the radio, listen to anything playing or talking, as long as it was noise.

Conrad loaned him books, and he was amazed at how much company they were. He had never read much before, just some little *Reader's Digest* things, but he found the Westerns soothing. Most of them were by someone called Louis L'Amour, and there were older ones that he liked even better by someone called Luke Short, and sometimes the books were not Westerns, but were about men with blazing machine guns who killed lots of other men, then got lots of pussy and flew off in planes on their way to other adventures. He wondered if you could really get a job like those guys had, and what the requirements for hiring were.

But, TV or not, radio or not, books or not, as night moved on toward sleep, he would begin to feel ill at ease. He began to think of the Ice Man all over again.

On nights when he couldn't sleep for thinking about it, he'd go outside. Outside usually being some pasture or park area Frost had arranged for them to stay in, and he'd look at the sky and all about, trying to make some sort of plan, but never making one, and being confused on what he should make a plan about anyway. His last plan had certainly been a doozy. A plan like that made you hold back on future arrangements.

It was on his first late night of doing this that he discovered Conrad lying on top of Frost's trailer. He was a fair distance away, his back to Bill, and he lay still, his ear to the roof. At first Bill thought he was up there eavesdropping, trying to catch the sound of lustful breathing inside, or listen to the mousesqueak rhythm of bed springs.

But, as he became accustomed to the dark, Bill saw that Conrad lay with his head on a pillow, and there was a blanket stretched over him. He was sleeping there, like a pet near its master, waiting for tidbits, soon to be called, tucked in for the night with a dream and a razor.

Bill's first thought was: What if it rains? Where does he sleep then? Underneath? Does he have a basket there? A bowl?

But it never seemed to rain anymore, not since that day it had cooled his mosquito-wounded face. It was hot with a constant savage wind blowing, the air so brittle a wave of your hand might knock a crack in it.

Every night when Bill came out of his trailer unable to sleep, there was Conrad. On occasion the trailer would be rocking to the lovemaking of the two inside, and above them, on the rooftop, Conrad would be sleeping, as content as a baby in a wind-up swing.

It got so watching Conrad was a kind of diversion. Late nights, Bill would sneak out and around the side and get in a place where he could see Frost's trailer.

On occasion Conrad would not be there, but more often than not he was. One night Conrad was there, and so was the bearded lady. She had her hefty self on all fours and her dress pushed up over her ample ass and her panties around one ankle. Conrad, naked except for his hind leg shoes, was mounting her, proving that he did indeed do it doggie style.

The bearded woman's head was tossed back, and the way her beard stuck out she looked like those pictures Bill had seen of the Sphinx. Conrad was so eager with his work on the bearded lady's white round ass, he looked not unlike a child wrestling a beach ball about to roll out from under him. In time Conrad settled down, got his bearings, and the motor home began to rock with a tidelike motion. Bill figured the bearded lady and Conrad were working to the rhythm of the humping of the Frost couple inside; a four-some sharing the same sexual cadence if not the same space.

Bill watched this with a kind of amazement. Eventually the bearded lady lifted her head even more and pointed her beard at the moon and gave out a grunt he could hear, and Conrad, shaking like a convict taking his voltage in the electric chair, came to a finish. They lay down together, and Conrad pulled a blanket over them. But the motor home rocked on, Frost either taking long to finish or striving for a double.

The whole thing made Bill lonely as the last pig in a slaughterhouse line.

Bill resented Conrad got to drive the Ice Man's trailer. This was obviously an important assignment. He, instead, had been given Frost's motor home to drive. At first he thought this was an honor, but in time he realized the Ice Man was, at least to Frost, the most important member of the carnival, and he trusted it only to Conrad, his number one man. Dog. Whatever. Trusted it to him even if he had to pull the trailer while sitting on a cushion, working the pedals with a stick.

Bill soon lost his resentment, however, and learned to take pride in his responsibility. Gidget had taken to staying in bed while he drove instead of riding with Frost or driving the car. She liked to sleep until they came to the next town and set up. At that point she would abandon the camper for air and cigarettes, always dressed in shorts and T-shirts too small to hold her.

She never did any work that Bill could see, outside of what she did at night with Frost in their bed. Perhaps she saw this as work enough. Bill knew, had he been Gidget, he'd have certainly counted it as a full-time job with overtime. Maybe a little hazard pay for having to deal with that extra hand.

Bill enjoyed having Gidget in the motor home while he drove. He could smell her, even when he was behind the wheel and she slept behind the closed bedroom door. It was a smell rich and wet, like a lathered horse.

One morning he liked it even more. They were driving to a small town called Gladewater, planning to set up just outside near what Frost called "a row of honkeytonks."

On the dash of the motor home was a mirror Gidget used to apply makeup to her eyes and lips and brush her hair. He looked at it to examine his face, and liked what he saw. A face clear of swelling and strangeness. Not a bad-looking face, a good-looking face actually, the one thing about himself of which he could be proud, yet had nothing to do with. Nature had given it to him, not out of design he figured, but in the manner a blackjack dealer might turn over a card and find a King.

Still, accident or heavenly design, it was his face, and it was almost back to normal, just tired and a little splotched.

But what interested Bill even more than his face was that the mirror showed him the reflection of the now open bedroom door behind him. In the doorway, sleepy-headed, hair tangled, was Gidget. She was naked as the day she was born, but certainly a lot better looking than at that earlier moment, and she was struggling into a pair of blue jean shorts, wrestling the denim with the fervor of a rodeo rider trying to bulldog a steer, throwing her soft butt back and forth like a pendulum, giving him a wiggling peek at other charms, wobbling boobs, legs long and soft and brown and popped with muscle, a dark V of fuzz coating what Eve used to destroy Adam. Apple, hell. Everyone knew what it was Adam wanted and why he did what he did. A woman like that, like Eve, like Gidget, she could make you set fire to an old folks home and beat the survivors over the head with a shovel as they ran out. A woman like that damn sure wouldn't have to do much to get some guy to steal an apple.

Much to Bill's disappointment, Gidget eventually slid into the shorts and straightened up. She turned and looked toward the front of the motor home where he manned the wheel. He could tell from the set of her face that she knew he was looking at her in the mirror. The shorts were unzipped all the way down, and he could see the crease of the beast itself. Her breasts were revealed, and she made no effort to cover herself. Slowly, she leaned forward and took hold of the sliding bedroom door. Her breasts fell forward, as if about to dive-bomb from her chest and bounce his way. Then she pulled the door closed.

Bill caught his breath and brought the motor home back between the lines.

About fifteen minutes later, for the first time in over a month, it began to rain. Gently at first, then a real gully-washer.

Eighteen

Couple days later, one night after the suckers had left, Bill, unable to sleep, as usual, was outside the Ice Man's trailer pissing in the dirt. He could have pissed inside in the toilet, but here he was out in the night with an urge to go. It was a cool night, still damp from all the rain they had been getting, and there was a low fog over everything. Bill felt as if he were in a bottle with a cotton stopper, like those killing bottles they used for bugs, where you put the bug in and soaked the cotton in alcohol or something and stuck it in the bottle top and the bug died from the fumes.

There were still some lights left on from the carnival and there were a couple porch lights burning on trailers, and everything looked hot out there, even if it wasn't. The whirligig had not been dismantled, and wouldn't be until tomorrow. It looked like a wheel that had come off one of God's toys and been forgotten.

Bill could hear the two-headed nigger playing juke and soul music tapes in their trailer. They did that a lot and sometimes turned it up too loud and had to be gotten on to, but tonight he could hear it and it was just loud enough and he liked the song. "Soul Man."

He listened while he drained his lizard, then packed up and was about to step inside and crack open a J.D. Hardin Western book with fucking in it, when the tune changed and the music cranked up with the Isley Brothers singing "Shout." He listened to that a few seconds, then the two-headed nigger's trailer door burst open and the two-headed nigger danced out.

Or sort of danced. Bill couldn't rightly decide if it was dancing. He, or they, were falling all over the pasture, dipping here, jerking there. Two pea brains caught up in rhythms that a single body couldn't define.

They tried to go different ways and the heads were singing and weren't very good at it. Eventually they fell down in the pasture and ended up doing what they did at meals, writhing in the wet grass, screaming and yelling, slapping at each other with their hands, causing as much damage to themselves by striking as by getting hit. They sounded drunk.

The yelling and the music popped heads out of trailers, and Bill saw one of the heads was U.S. Grant. She was in a short nightie, and she was standing in a crack in the door, looking out to see what was going on. Bill could see a face behind her, lit up by the little porch light on her trailer. It was Phil of the Constant Half-Hard Dick. His head seemed to be floating just behind her shoulder, like a helium-filled balloon on a string. Phil's arm was visible too, around U.S. Grant's ample waist. He probably thought he couldn't be seen, but Bill could see him.

And so could Conrad.

Due to the rain, Conrad had not been at his post on top of Frost's trailer. Where he had been Bill was uncertain, but Conrad suddenly crossed the gap between the Pickled Punk trailer and U.S. Grant's trailer; the music and the yelling had stirred him the way it had everyone else.

Conrad loped on all fours up the steps to U.S. Grant's trailer and between her legs, knocking her backwards inside. In the next instant there was a bloodcurdling scream and Phil came leaping out of the trailer butt naked, a gash in his buttock, his greasy hair rolling all over his head. Blood flew out of the wound as he hopped and the drops seemed to rise up in slow motion and hang in place and become like jewels in the odd cotton-covered night and the carnival lights, then the drops fell and exploded in the damp grass.

Bill couldn't help but note Phil's pecker wasn't half hard. He could tell that even from a distance. You couldn't even see it, it was such a peanut. The cool air, the fact that a dog with a razor was flying out of an open trailer door after him wasn't something to give it much size either.

"You sonofabitch," Conrad said, "I'm gonna make you look like a highway map."

Phil nimbly leaped and hopped and avoided the slashing razor. "We weren't doin' nothin'! Jest watchin' TV."

"Naked!"

Conrad flashed the razor again and Phil screamed and jumped back and Conrad jumped with him and the razor went out and then Phil was trying to fight back by kicking. Next thing they were both down in the dirt and Conrad was on top with the razor raised.

Bill thought it was just as good Phil hadn't gone into the money collection racket. He wasn't worth a shit at intimidation. In a moment they'd have to get someone fresh to run the whirligig and Conrad would be on his way to doing about three hundred years in prison, or maybe, like a dog nobody wanted, he might get put to sleep by law enforcement.

Out of nowhere Frost appeared. He was in his white silk shorts, and his skin was white in the light and his head was whiter yet. Bill could see the hand on his chest, flopping about as Frost moved, as if it were signaling directions. It was a dark hand now, like it had been dipped in black paint.

Frost had hold of Conrad's neck. To Bill's amazement, he picked Conrad up, jerked him up so hard the razor flew from his hand. Conrad flailed about. Phil jumped up, and seeing an opening, he kicked Conrad in one of his dangling legs.

Frost's free hand shot out and caught Phil by the back of the neck as well. He pulled him forward, slammed Phil and Conrad together and dropped them unconscious to the ground. Frost took a deep breath, stood over them like a stern god. Bill, who had eased forward, saw the hand on Frost's chest was dark because it wore a thin black glove.

U.S. Grant was out of her trailer in a flash. She sat down on the wet grass, took hold of Conrad's head, put it in her lap, and stroked his snout. Phil moaned a little. Bill, and most everyone else in the carnival, stood over him and looked at his nakedness. Even Double Buckwheat was there, their music still playing in the background. "A Lover's Question" now.

Yep, a peanut, Bill thought. Everyone from the pinheads to the pumpkin heads to the assorted freaks were nodding and mumbling about the same thing. They had all heard the story.

Frost bent down and looked at Conrad. Conrad's eyes

113

blinked. Frost said, "Sorry, boy. I can't let you kill some-one." Then to Phil: "Phil, get something around you and come to my trailer. I'll patch up those cuts. If it's bad, we'll take you to the emergency room."

"Cuts ain't bad," Phil said, pushing his hair back with his hand, flicking his wrist to remove grease from his fingers. "Not that fuckin' Butch the Show Dog here didn't try."

Conrad jerked as if to get up, but Frost pushed a palm in his chest and Conrad fell back into U.S. Grant's lap. She stroked his head and said, "Sorry, Conrad. I'm so, so, so sorry."

"Were y'all . . . fuckin'?"

"Yes. But it wasn't any good. He wasn't any good. I'm so, so sorry."

"You wasn't no good neither," Phil said. "It didn't mat-ter which beard I was pokin'. It was the same bad."

"You took him in your mouth?" Conrad said.

"It didn't go in far," she said. "There wasn't enough of it to reach the back of my throat." .

Conrad groaned. Phil cussed and said, "It's just cold is all. It wasn't cold you'd see some dick, that's what I'm tryin' to tell you."

One of Double Buckwheat's heads said, "That ain't no half-hard dick." The other said, "We got dicks bigger'n that."

"Go to hell," Phil said, getting up.

"It didn't mean nothing," U.S. Grant said to Conrad, stroking his head. "It didn't mean a thing."

Conrad made a sound in his throat like someone trying to swallow a golf ball. U.S. Grant tried to help him to his feet, but couldn't quite do it, and Conrad didn't have the will to manage.

Bill went over and got Conrad onto all fours. Conrad

nodded at him, then without a word he and U.S. Grant made for her trailer. She had a big patch of mud and grass on the back of her nightgown, and Bill was surprised to find himself feeling sorry for her. He had never really thought he could be concerned with a bearded lady's problems.

Conrad looked like he'd just been in the dogfight to end all dogfights, but his head was up, and he looked proud enough to drop his pants, lift a leg, and piss on a trailer tire. Instead he went up and inside and U.S. Grant closed the door.

Frost put a hand on Bill's shoulder. "Good man," he said.

Bill felt a warmth rise inside him. It was a feeling he didn't entirely understand.

"You boys," Frost said to Double Buckwheat, "turn off that music and go to bed. And you've been drinkin', I can tell. Tomorrow, we get rid of all your booze. You two can't drink. You know that."

"We can we want to," said one head.

Frost gave him a look. The other head replied promptly, "But we don't want to."

"Better," Frost said.

The music playing now was "Blue Moon," and "the boys" followed its notes into their trailer, closed the door, and just as the Temptations began to sing "Can't Get Next to You," the music went off.

Bill watched Frost head back to his trailer, the hand flapping, his huge white body floating across the wet night grass. He saw Gidget standing in the doorway of the motor home, framed by a light from inside. She had on a pair of panties so brief they might have been made out of strip of black Christmas ribbon. You could see the dark outline of blond hair trimming the edges of the cloth. She wore a matching top that only went over the tops of her breasts. The smooth bottoms of her breasts were like two beautiful moons dipping out of cloud cover. She stared at Bill, then went inside.

Frost went up the steps and into the trailer. A moment later, Phil, with a towel around his waist and bleeding from his superficial wounds, went after him, looking for all the world like a boy on his way to the principal's office. As he passed, Bill said, "Reckon when you jumped out of that trailer something rejogged your brain."

"What?"

"Knocked something loose in there so you don't have to suffer from a half-hard dick all the time."

"Fuck you."

"What with?"

Phil was defeated now, his head dropped another degree toward his chest. It was obvious he wouldn't be able to collect money from deadbeats and no one was wondering about the size of his half-hard dick anymore. He couldn't even control U.S. Grant the bearded lady, didn't have enough dick to fill her mouth, so how was he going to run a string of whores? It was the whirligig and hair grease for him, and that was it.

Nineteen

Next morning it was discovered the whirligig was still in place, but the whirligig owner was not. Phil had departed in his truck and trailer without bothering to take the ride with him.

Before decamping Phil had decided on a change of career after all. He had broken into the Pickled Punk trailer, causing the fold-out wall to collapse, exposing the interior to the light of day and the population of the carnival.

Phil had departed with all the Punks, forty-eight dollars and fifty-two cents of bread and egg money, a canned ham, and two bags of M&Ms. With the exception of the Punks, all this belonged to Conrad, who Bill discovered lived in the Pickled Punk trailer with a small refrigerator, a hot plate, a pallet on the floor, a greasy pillow, and a wrinkled magazine picture of Jesus's face taped to the wall.

The picture was one of those where Jesus was on the cross, but you couldn't see the cross or his body, just the face. The face looked swollen. There was a crown of thorns on his head, tears on his cheeks, blood leaking down from his forehead. The picture looked to have been wadded up at one time and straightened out, maybe with an iron. In the harsh sunlight all the little creases made the Savior look not only in pain, but old and tired and disappointed, as well as in need of a good sunlamp. On the floor next to Conrad's pallet were scattered playing cards. One of them, a Joker, was turned face up and had a heel print on it, presumably Phil's.

"It ain't much, but I call it home," Conrad said. He sat by Bill's side smoking a cigarette. The pinheads and Double Buckwheat were behind them, peeking into the ravaged room that had been home to Conrad and assorted fucked-up babies in alcohol.

"You ought to not have to sleep on the floor," Bill said.

"I don't have to," Conrad said. "It's what I like. Some reason, messed up like I am, a bed doesn't work as well. I get some serious backaches, and a chiropractor doesn't know what to do with me. I think they figure I ought to go to a vet. I sleep on the floor or on the roof of Frost's motor home. It's the most comfortable of the trailers and such."

The pinheads and Double Buckwheat grew bored looking at the pallet, the picture, and the empty space where the Punks had been, so they wandered off.

"Hey, thanks for helping me last night."

"That wasn't anything. I just helped you up."

"It was enough . . . Hell, I don't blame her."

"Beg pardon?"

"She couldn't help herself. She wanted something normal. I reckon I had a normal woman would go to bed with me, I'd go. Even if she was ugly enough to have to sneak up on a glass of water. It'd make me feel like I wasn't on the outside lookin' in. Like I was just another fella out there doin' what other fellas did. I was mad last night, but I forgive her. I don't take it personal. You can't take something like that personal."

Bill felt he could, but he changed the subject, nodded at the picture on the wall. "I see you're religious."

"Just liked the picture. Kid wadded it up and tossed it at me one night. Out of curiosity, I unwadded it and it was that guy. It being up there on the wall makes me feel I got company. Play myself a game of cards now and then, I try to imagine he's playin' against me and the Pickled Punks are watchin'. You know, bunch of interested bystanders watching two card sharpies work. I have to take it off the wall when the Punks are on display . . . Were on display . . . Damn, I'm gonna miss them M&Ms. And that forty dollars or so is all I've been able to save. I spend too much money on those damn M&Ms. They're kind of like catnip to me. And U.S. Grant likes 'em."

Out of the corner of his eye Bill could see Conrad's eyes had watered up. Without really knowing he was going to do it, he reached out and patted Conrad on the shoulder.

Conrad coughed and looked at the ground. To give him a semblance of privacy, Bill looked out at the whirligig. The cottony fog was rapidly being burned off by the heat of the morning sun and already deep shadows were forming around it. Wasn't long, though, before black clouds, like skin cancers, began to appear on the face of the sky, and off in the distance was a rumbling sound like a hungry belly wanting to be filled.

*   *   *

Frost had to go into the nearest town to talk to the police and try and get something done about Phil. In the meantime, it became necessary to move on to the next location. The whirligig was left where it was and other things were loaded up. Bill got behind the wheel of the motor home, Gidget in the back, sleeping as usual.

Bill was the last in the caravan line. The stretch of highway the caravan took was littered with clapboard houses, black kids in yards that were mostly made of gravel, sunburned grass, and nasty-looking chickens. Bill drove past at least six burned-out filling stations, half of them with the pumps pulled up, leaving only the concrete structures they had stood on and the steel rods they had been fastened to.

They hit a wide four-lane stretch of highway, and Bill was thinking maybe things weren't working out so bad after all. He was sort of getting used to the carnival. All the freaks were starting to look regular to him, and he fit in here good as he fit in anywhere. Better maybe. He had discovered he could talk to Conrad in a way that was different from the way he had talked to Fat Boy and Chaplin.

The bedroom door slid open and Gidget, wearing green silk shorts and a matching pajama top that had only one button near the center, came barefoot up to the front and sat in the passenger's seat. The seat swiveled and she turned it toward Bill and crossed her legs way over and looked at him with that pouty look of hers that made Bill want to slap her one moment and fuck her the next.

"They find Phil?"

"Not yet. Frost went to town to see about it."

"What town?"

"One near where we was."

"You mean the other direction?"

"Yeah."

"He ain't in the caravan?"

"No."

Gidget took a quiet moment to consider this. She looked at herself in the mirror on the dash, seemed to like what she was looking at. She flicked her hair and turned her attention back to Bill.

"You know, you look like James Dean some. Only with darker hair."

"The sausage guy?"

"Who?"

"Sells sausage. He used to be a country singer."

"I don't know who that is . . . James Dean, the movie star."

"Never heard of him."

"*East of Eden*. *Giant*. He got killed in a car wreck."

"Jimmy Dean is who I know of. He sells sausage. They ain't bad. I don't know if he got killed in a car wreck or not."

"I don't care about any sausages."

"You brought it up."

"I said you looked like James Dean the movie star, I didn't say anything about any sausages. I can't believe you don't know who James Dean is."

"Yeah, well I can't believe you don't know who Jimmy Dean is. He's on TV all the time and he sells sausage."

"James Dean's on the TV too. In old movies."

"I don't watch movies much."

"Well, you're missin' out. I grew up on the TV set. I might as well, wasn't nothing else to do. My Mama and I used to watch it together, late at night. She'd come stay in my room and we'd watch TV. That was when my step-daddy was drunk and wanted to hit her. She said I was named after a movie she liked about a girl named Gidget. You know it?"

Bill shook his head.

"Reckon you don't know who James Dean is, there's a damn good chance you aren't gonna know about a movie called *Gidget*. Anyway, she said she and my Daddy saw it on TV once, and she said something about it made her feel romantic, and they made love and I was conceived. They had to get married on account of me. Daddy said my Mama was a bitch from hell and I was her little bitch. He always said that, like we weren't human."

"What happened to him? Your Daddy?"

"He stuck his head out a car window and got hit by a signpost. Mama was drivin'. She said she didn't even know he'd gotten hit. He rolled down his window and stuck his head out and she said she heard a whack, and he just sat back down in the car with his head turned, and she didn't think nothing of it. Talked to him for five miles she said, before she realized he wasn't answering any of her questions and he smelled like shit. See, when he got hit he crapped himself. It wasn't his fault, it's just your muscles and your bowels let go when you get killed sudden like."

"Why in hell was he stickin' his head out of a car window?"

"Mama said he always did that. Like a dog. He thought it was funny. But she was drivin' too close to the side that day and that sign got him. I finally ended up seeing that movie."

"What movie?"

"*Gidget*. I finally saw it, and it sucked. Wasn't nothin' in there would make me want to fuck anybody. Not just seein' the movie, anyway. I figure what Mom did was fuck through the movie and she just noticed it was on and remembered the name of it. Had to be like that, 'cause there isn't anything hot about that movie. Not to me anyway. Some people can get turned on by all manner of things. But I was named after the girl in there. Her movie name anyway. Gidget."

Bill thought he ought to leave well enough alone, but he couldn't help himself. "You wasn't talkin' to me before, why are you friendly now?"

"You aren't as scary-lookin'. I see enough freaks in this carnival, I don't want to have to make friends with 'em. I set out to be a model, not a freak show owner's wife."

"What happened to the modelin'?"

"Too much tits and ass and not enough legs and neck."

"I don't know that's so bad."

"Yeah?"

"Looks all right."

"All right. Hell, you'd cut off one of your feet if you thought you was gonna get your thang in me. I may not know much, but I know men."

"You know so much, you don't like freaks so much, how come you're married to one?"

"You're not nice. I thought maybe you was nice 'cause you looked nice, but you aren't. And now that I can see better in the light, you don't look that much like James Dean anyway."

She tried to appear mad but Bill didn't think she was all that upset. She went back to the bedroom and shut the door.

Bill felt as if he'd been run over by a truck. He sucked in the air. It was full of her perfume, and she hadn't been wearing any. She was right, he'd cut off his goddamn foot.

Twenty

Bill drove on, thinking about Gidget. By midday it was starting to get dark. The air was heavy and the clouds looked like swollen bladders. Zippers of lightning pulled their flies above the pines, exposing hot light.

Then Bill saw a remarkable thing. In the distance, down the flat stretch of highway, there was a patch darker than anywhere else. It looked as if one of the clouds had set down on the ground, and it was smooth and round and rolling toward him, like a bowling ball.

When the cloud hit it was solid with wind and rain. The strike made the motor home slide and the steering wheel was useless. The home rattled and rocked and Bill heard Gidget yell and hit the wall in the bedroom.

The motor home went way right off the road, between two scrubby pine trees. It dipped in a ditch, came out of it because the other side was lower. It went up and out and along the grass and mounted a concrete offshoot, just missed a metal picnic table, then managed to hit something else.

By the time Bill got it together he realized he was situated under a cluster of large oak trees in a roadside park. The front of the vehicle had gone off the concrete and hit a sign with a historical marker on it.

He left the motor running and turned on the windshield wipers. The motor home was shaking violently. A bolt of lightning hit one of the oaks and knocked a limb about the size of a telephone pole loose and slammed it on the ground in front of the motor home. There was another limb sticking off the larger limb, and it brushed over the front and touched the roof, dripping leaves onto the windshield.

Gidget came stumbling from the bedroom cussing. "You sonofabitch," she said. "Can't you drive?"

"Not in this," Bill said. He put the motor home in gear and eased back in his seat and watched the storm through the windshield and the gaps in the leaves draped over it. Outside, debris in the form of leaves, dirt, limbs, and rubbish was being tossed about in the manner a dryer tosses clothes.

"Good God," Gidget said. "We in a tornado?"

"We got hit by what looked like a ball of black wind. I reckon we're on the edge of a tornado."

Lightning cracked its whip and the interior of the motor home was charged with electricity. Bill felt his nose hairs wiggle.

"God almighty," Gidget said. She took the passenger's seat, watching the storm, shivering. There was a pack of cigarettes and a lighter in the little tray on the dash, and she took them and held them in her lap, then nervously re-turned them.

Bill was looking out the side window, through some trees and down a dip of land toward the highway. There was a whipping sound and he saw something pop yellow light, then the light was flicking toward him. He realized it was a high-line wire that had snapped free and been thrown up high over the trees. It dropped across an oak limb and fell like a fishing line tipped with an electric eel. The end of the line popped and fizzled and writhed and danced on the cement near the motor home.

Gidget screamed and jumped out of her seat and onto Bill's lap. She hugged him around the neck. He found his hand had come up under her pajama top and was resting on the smooth skin at the small of her back. The flesh there was warm and damp with sweat. She looked at him and swallowed. Her eyes were big, the pupils swollen. She held him tighter. She looked at the popping high-line wire.

"That scared me."

"It didn't do me no good neither."

"Maybe you ought to cut off the windshield wipers. Not like we're goin' nowhere, and it could get hung up with some of those leaves."

Easing forward, careful to hold Gidget on his knee, Bill shut off the windshield wipers. Without their beating sound it was quiet inside the motor home. Outside was the wind, the rain, and the sputtering high-line wire.

"We could have been killed, had that wire hit the motor home," she said.

"I reckon."

"We'd have been electrocuted, wouldn't we?"

"I don't know. Maybe this thing's insulated enough."

"No, we'd have been killed. We aren't that far from

127

death right now. That wind turned, it could throw that wire on us."

"I'll try to back out from under this limb."

Gidget didn't move so he could try it. "Death is all around us. It always is, you know?"

"I reckon."

"Ain't nothing to reckon. It is. Sometimes it takes a certain moment to let you know."

Gidget's face came close to his. Her breath was sweet. Without really thinking about it, his hand dropped and came to rest on the top of her ass, which was damp through the thin green cloth.

"Just one change in the wind and that wire moving some," she said, "our whole life would be over."

She leaned closer and he kissed her and she bit his bottom lip, hard enough to draw blood. When she leaned back from him she was smiling and there was blood on her lips. She unbuttoned her top.

"What about everybody else?" Bill said.

"They aren't here. They're out there in the storm too. A little luck, and they'll get blown away."

"What about Frost?"

"He's got a hand on his chest."

She pushed at the edges of the pajama top and showed him her breasts.

"Jesus," he said. He moved his hands up the front of her and pushed her top off and took hold of her breasts. "Excellent."

"Hell, baby. They're better than that."

He put a nipple in his mouth and sucked. There was a tinge of sweat on her body, and it tasted the way she smelled. He moved from one nipple to the other, then back to her face. He kissed her, tasting his own blood. She rose up and came out of her panties and straddled his knees, leaving room to use her hand on his crotch. Soon he was out of his clothes and they were on the floor and she was on top of him. He thought: Hell, what am I doing? Frost ain't done nothing to me and this is his wife.

Electricity crackled outside and the wind moaned and the motor home shook. In a flash of light he got a good look at Gidget's face. In that moment it was harsh, her lips blue, her eyes the color of wet aluminum.

They rolled across the floor and he came out on top between her legs and mounted her. As he entered her he realized he was yet another man consumed by the mystery that destroyed Adam.

Eventually they finished and lay on the floor together, she in the crook of his arm with her hand on his chest. The sky had grown blacker and the rain was knocking all over the motor home. Occasionally the dark outside would brighten up from the lightning or the spitting electric wire. Bill had lost his nervousness. He felt protected by the storm now, as if it were keeping out the world and hiding them in their metal cocoon.

"I don't see why you married Frost if you don't like him and you don't like the carnival and the freaks."

"You ever been so you couldn't get out of something?"

"I think I have."

"Then you got to know what I mean. I wanted to be a model, but I didn't have the right build. I have this build men like but magazines don't."

"I told you how I feel about it."

"That's how all men feel about it that don't prefer to suck dick."

Bill couldn't get away from thoughts of the Old Testament. "Reckon yours is the kind of body Eve had."

"I'm not sure you mean that as a compliment, buster. Eve always gets considered bad."

"She fucked up the world. Brought sin into it."

"Like Adam isn't at fault for being stupid. If anyone fucked up the world, it was him. He didn't think with the right head. Men don't ever think with the right head."

"Yeah, but the big head don't ever get to feel as good as the little head when it's doing its kind of thinking."

"I fucked a preacher once. He was going to save me and he gave me special Bible lessons. I was sixteen. He showed me what Adam and Eve had done as an object lesson. It taught me some things all right. He had a big ole wart on the head of his dick. That's really a plus, it hits the right spot. Other than that he showed me preachers don't know any more than Adam did, and never will. God with all his goodness doesn't know what he's up against. Bad is good, baby."

"You still ain't told me why you married Frost and took up with the carnival."

"When the modeling didn't work out, and my Mama died, I didn't have anything to go back to. My stepfather had come to like me better as I got older, and not because he wanted to talk about what he could do for me as a daughter. He didn't never do anything, but I could tell he wanted to. He had the same look as that goddamn preacher, and I figured he didn't even have a well-placed wart on his dick, and I damn sure didn't want to find out.

"So I didn't go home again 'cause there wasn't any home to go to. I went out to Los Angeles, maybe thinking I'd be seen by one of those producers or directors or an actor or something, and get in the movies. I couldn't act, but I figured I could look good. I was ready to fuck my way to the top, or even to the middle. I got fucked by a lot said they could get me in the movies, but closest I got to it was a movie date and a little feel-up while I was in the dark.

"I worked some restaurants and cafes but didn't care for that either. I got a job working in this place with a glass you strip behind and you do things you're asked by a customer talks to you over a microphone and puts money down. They always want you to spread your pussy. It comes to that eventually. You can dance, you can wiggle, but it's going to turn out you got to use your fingers like a salad spoon. They're gonna ask for that come hell or high water, like they're gonna see a place in there better than this one. And even if they did, I don't get it. They're still on the outside looking in.

"I made some good money, but you can't imagine how tired you get of trying to look like nothing makes you happier than to have some guy jerking his gherkin on the other side of the glass. You wouldn't believe the nasty ole dicks I've seen through that glass. I gave it up. Wasn't any future to it. I came back to East Texas and found there wasn't any future here either. I was back to working cafes and such and not liking it much. I made a few dollars after hours in the back seats of cars, but that wasn't any way to go.

"I got in with this guy did forgery for a while, and I learned how to duplicate handwriting and cash hot checks and money orders. It was all right, but he got caught and I almost did, so I gave that up."

"You can write like someone else, that what you mean?"

"I can write like a lot of folks. The simpler the signature is, harder time I have with it. Easiest way to do it is turn the signature upside down and try to draw it. But it's a crummy racket. You can only run that one for so long. I got out of it.

"I went to work at a Mexican restaurant over in Tyler and this carnival come through and Frost came to eat there and he was nice to me and tipped me good. He told me about the carnival, and you know, I thought it was some kind of circus. I didn't know there was a difference. It wasn't that smelling elephant shit was any more appealing, but it sounded a bit more romantic than pinheads, bearded ladies, and dog-men.

"Six months later he come through again, and I could tell he had the hots for me, you know, but he wasn't trying nothing. Wasn't trying to get me in the back seat of a car or in a motel room. He was nice. I hadn't seen a lot of nice. I thought nice might be pretty good. Third time he came through he asked me to marry him. Just like that. It was kind of sweet. Pathetic, but sweet. And I'd come to hate the smell of an enchilada. I couldn't get that smell off of me. I'd be away from work, doing something else, the wind would change, and I smelled like a Number 3 Dinner."

"What was on that dinner?"

"Two tacos, an enchilada, a tamale, beans and rice. You got free tortillas and you had to order a drink separate. It was a hell of a deal if you wanted it. Three ninety-eight plus tax and a tip."

"I bet you got plenty of tips."

"If there was a man at the table I did. I knew how to work that. You serve the dinner close with your tits on their shoulders and you wear your dress just a little short and wear shoes with tall heels and walk so they notice it. I can talk real sweet too, Bill. You want to hear sweet, I'm a goddamn songbird."

"So you married Frost to get away from Mexican dinners?"

"Pretty much. And he seemed sweet, you know. I didn't marry him with plans of not staying married. I was going through my 'I want a home and family' stage. Maybe I still want that. But I didn't know he had a hand on his chest and that I'd be living with a bunch of retarded pinheads and genetic fuck-ups. And he's so goddamn good he gives me the creeps. I like a man with a bit more devil in him."

"The freaks ain't so bad, you get to know them."

"I don't want to know 'em. I want some little piece of the fairy tale, Bill."

"Well, I don't guess you're talkin' about me."

"I might be."

"'Cause we fucked?"

"'Cause you was a frog that turned into a prince. All ugly and swole up, and then you turned into James Dean, and don't start that shit about the sausage again."

"I ain't got any idea about James Dean."

"Wait a minute," she said, and got up and went into the bedroom and came back carrying a book. She turned on a light over the sink. "Come here."

Bill got off the floor and went over and looked at the page she had the book turned to. It was a picture of a guy stretched out on the hood of a truck.

"That's him in *Giant*."

Bill thought: Goddamn, I do look like him.

She turned pages. There were more pictures. He really did look like this guy, only with darker hair and a little longer face. Maybe more nose.

"Well," she said.

"We favor," he said.

"You're taller-looking than him. I like you taller."

She closed the book and Bill looked at the cover. *The Pictorial James Dean*. She lay the book next to the kitchen sink and turned and kissed him. His lip was still sore where she had bit him. She sucked at the wound. Her tongue found his and they lay on the floor again and did it. Gidget on top.

Twenty-one

Whenthe storm passed and the sun came out it grew re-
markably calm. Gidget picked up her book and her clothes
and went back to the bedroom and locked the door without so much as a kiss my ass. It was like it had never happened, but it had. Bill was raw and sore from what they had
been doing.

Bill dressed, went outside and tried to move the big
limb, but couldn't do it. He figured if he kept trying his
only reward would be a strained nut. He did pause, however, to read the historical marker. It told how this had
once been the site of an unsuccessful cannonball factory.

He backed the motor home completely onto the concrete drive, and carefully backed down it, being sure to stay
away from the high-line wire. The motor home was big and
having to use only mirrors made it hard, but he got it out
of there and finally on the highway. He drove onward,

looking for other members of the carnival. He found the Ice Man's trailer and truck cab in a ditch. The cab was centered in the ditch in about two feet of water, and the trailer was partially in and partially jackknifed to the right where the end of it had knocked a gap in a barbed wire fence and smashed a small pine tree.

Conrad was sitting in the truck behind the steering wheel smoking a cigarette. There was about a pack's worth of butts floating in the ditch water by the truck. On the seat beside him was the rig he fastened to his leg when he was driving.

Bill pulled over, climbed in the ditch, looked in the open driver's window. Conrad gave him a doggie grin and flicked ash into the ditch water. Bill noted that the front of Conrad's clothes were wet, and he looked uncomfortable. "I'm glad to see you. Figured I got out of the car, some redneck liked to run over dogs would veer off the highway and get me. I wanted to lay down. After an hour or so, that's more comfortable than trying to sit like this, but I figured I laid down, I might miss one of our group they came by in the rain. I wanted to be ready to honk my horn and flash my lights. Then the sun came out and I didn't lay down either. I decided to smoke cigarettes. I didn't even see you come up."

"You just stuck?"

"I think so. Wind shoved me off the road."

"I don't think I can pull it out, even if I had a chain."

"Nope. It's a wrecker job. A big wrecker."

"What about the Ice Man?"

"He's all right. I checked on him first thing. Neither he nor the freezer moved an inch. That's why I'm all wet, going back there to check. I'm built low to the ground, you know." Conrad opened the door of the truck cab. "I hate to ask you this, but think you could lift me up? Otherwise, I'm going to have to walk through ditch water again. You go through it, it ain't gonna wash up and lick your belly."

"All right."

Bill let Conrad climb on his back. The dog-man was heavier than he expected. The idea of touching Conrad just a couple weeks ago would have made him feel queasy, but now it was nothing. They climbed up the side of the ditch and Bill sat Conrad down in front of the motor home.

"Looks like you clipped the front a bit."

"Yeah. I hit a historical marker in a roadside park. Damn near got hit by a falling high-line wire."

"And how's the Princess?"

"She's all right."

"Yeah, well anyone's all right, you can bet it'll be her."

Bill and Conrad went inside the motor home and Conrad got up in the passenger chair. Bill noted that Conrad was sniffing the air. He wondered if he could smell what he and Gidget had been doing. He'd had his face in it for so long he couldn't smell anything but that, so he didn't know how the trailer smelled.

Bill started up the motor home, pulled onto the highway. As he drove along he tried to think of some kind of small talk to hand out to Conrad, but nothing came. If Conrad figured he'd been throwing the meat to the Princess, as he called her, and Bill sat silent, this was sure to feed the suspicion, but still, nothing came to him to say.

He thought: What if she comes out of there stark naked?

No, she wouldn't do that. She was bound to have looked out a window and seen what he was doing out there with Conrad, so she wouldn't come out.

But what if she hadn't seen, and she did come out? How

was he going to explain that? He thought maybe he should talk loud to Conrad so she could hear, but he still couldn't think of anything to say.

He looked at Conrad and Conrad was reaching Gidget's smokes off the dash and shaking one out. He used her lighter to light up. He sucked in the smoke and let some of it come out his nose and he opened his mouth and rolled his tongue in a funny way and smoke came out of there in the shape of a funnel and wreathed over his head and spread about in the motor home cabin.

"I don't hear nothing back there. You sure she's all right?"

"Sure. I talked to her earlier. She was all right then. She's maybe takin' a nap."

"A nap."

"Sure."

"You look a little ill, buddy."

"I'm tired. This storm and shit. It rattles the nerves."

"Yeah. Mine are rattled. I went off in that ditch so fast I didn't even know it till I was there. Sometimes, things like that happen. You're just going along, mindin' your own business, not expecting anything, then suddenly you're caught in a slide and you're off in a ditch."

"Yeah, that's right."

"You get out of the ditch, you got to have enough sense not to get back in it."

"Wasn't your fault in the first place."

"Maybe I wasn't alert enough. Wasn't like I didn't have a little warning. Thunderheads. Rain."

"It come pretty fast, that storm."

"Yeah. But I had some warning. I could sense it. You can sense a thing like that. The atmosphere is different. It's got a kind of electricity. A kind of smell. It's got an after-smell too."

"Yeah. But I didn't know anything. Just one minute I'm driving along, next minute I hit a post."

"Best thing to do in that case is back away from the post and drive off and keep on driving and stay away from posts in general."

Bill turned and looked at Conrad. "Yeah. I reckon you're right. That's what I'm doing, drivin' on."

Conrad nodded and smoked Gidget's cigarette. "That's a good idea, man. Me and U.S. Grant, we're tryin' to do the same. Drive on, you know? Stay out of ditches. Away from posts."

"And how are you doin'?"

"Well, it ain't easy. I think about it. What was goin' on and all with Phil, but we're doin' it. We got to do it. You got to look at the big picture. You look at it small, well, you're off in that ditch again, and maybe this next time the ditch is deeper and you can't climb out, not even with help. Savvy?"

"Sure."

A few miles farther they came upon U.S. Grant parked along the road on the opposite side, the cab turned in the opposite direction, trailer disconnected and sitting beside the road facing toward its original destination.

U.S. Grant had brought out a lawn chair and was seated in it next to her truck and trailer. The pin- and pumpkin heads had been riding with her and they were outside now, playing, running about and splashing in ditch water. Passing traffic slowed to look at this and wonder.

Bill looped around and went back and parked and he and Conrad got out. As soon as U.S. Grant saw Conrad she started crying and came out of her chair in a leap and grabbed him as if to pick him up like a pet. Instead she bent down and dropped a big hairy knee out from under her shift and rested it in the mud and hugged him.

"We spun around and the trailer snapped loose," she said. "I kept thinking I was gonna die and things weren't like they ought to be between us."

Conrad stroked her with his weird little hand. "It's all right."

"I didn't want to die with us not reconciled."

"We are. We're fine."

"What I done was wrong."

"I've already forgiven you. It won't happen again."

"I don't blame you for nothing."

The pinheads and the pumpkin heads were throwing dirt clods at one another.

"Bill," Conrad said, "I'm going to stay here with U.S. Grant. You go on to the next town and call in some wrecker service."

Conrad popped a snap on a back pocket and took out his razor and then his wallet. He removed a card. "This here is our road service. You use most anyone, we get a little discount. We can always use a discount. You call and tell them where we are, and they'll come. Tell them where my trailer is too. Any others you might see on the way in."

Bill took the card and Conrad replaced his wallet and razor and sat back on his haunches and shook Bill's hand. "You watch out for ditches now. There still might be some slick spots."

PART FOUR

A Feast of Possibilities

Twenty-two

Before Frost returned, wreckers did their work. Pinheads, pumpkin heads, a bearded lady, a dog-man, and the trailers were recovered. They were all brought to the designated place for the night. This place was a near a hill overlooking a clutch of willows fastened precariously by thin roots to red mud. The rain had swollen the river and turned it brown as a turd. There was a light wind, and the air tasted damp and smelled of fish.

Frost was cranky when he returned. He came into camp driving fast. He slammed the Chevy to a stop, throwing up mud and bogging the station wagon about halfway to the hubcaps. That made him even madder. He got out and kicked a tire, stomped about camp bellowing orders. When he heard about all that had happened, about the bang in his motor home, he put one hand on his hip and looked at the ground for a long time. Bill was standing nearby, Frost looked at him and frowned. "Wasn't anything you could do to keep this from happening?"

"It was the storm. I didn't start it."

"Don't be a smart-ass."

"What was I supposed to do?"

"You could have drove careful."

"It wasn't about driving. It was about a storm. It washed me off the road."

"Me too, Boss." It was Conrad. He suddenly appeared, waddling forward on all fours. He was wearing a pair of cuffed blue jeans and a red jersey, his odd shoes and hand protectors. "The Ice Man trailer was blown off the road, and me in it."

"Oh my God."

"It's all right, Boss. It didn't do nothing to it. U.S. Grant and some of the folks had a little adventure too. Everybody is okay. We're gonna have a wrecker bill, but that's all."

"You're sure?"

"Yeah. No one was hurt."

"Of course. Good. But I mean the Ice Man."

"He's fine. His hairs are all in place. I don't even think his dick swung to the other side."

"He's petrified. Nothing is going to swing."

"No shit?" Bill said.

Frost didn't answer. He went past Conrad, heading quickly for the Ice Man's trailer.

"I've never seen him like that," Bill said.

"Well, he gets like that when it comes to the carnival, and especially when it comes to the Ice Man. Normally he's all right, but now and then he'll go into a snit. This stuff

with Phil didn't do him any good neither. I always hated
Phil. He was more full of shit than a compost pile."

"Petrified? He said the Ice Man was petrified."

"That's what the man said."

"He don't look petrified."

"First I've heard of it, and I've known Frost for a long
time now, and he's always had the Ice Man exhibit. Then
again, I'm not that inquisitive about the Ice Man. Person-
ally, I don't fuck around with it. I don't care if he's petrified or putrefied. Hauling a dead body around seems crazy
to me. It ought to be buried. It gives me the willies."

"Try sleeping with him."

"Does he give good head?"

Bill turned and looked at Conrad, and slowly he smiled,
and they both laughed.

Late in the day, Frost gathered everyone in the center of
the camp and made a talk. A single cloud overhead dark-
ened and the dipping sun fell westward into the Sabine,
struggling as if about to drown, throwing out color like
yells for help.

"First off, I want to apologize for the way I came in here
today."

Mostly no one had noticed, but everyone nodded, more
out of respect that this was important to Frost, if not to
them.

"I was angry. I had to deal with the police. They found
Phil. He was drunk and parked in a truck stop, sleeping it
off in the cab of his trailer with a woman he had hired who
turned out to be man in a skirt, wig, and pantyhose."

"What color wig?" someone asked. Some snickers followed.

"In place of pressing charges we worked some things

out, me and Phil. He gave me the papers on his trailer, and the trailer of course. And the whirligig, which I've hired some men to load this very night. All of it will arrive here tomorrow morning—along with my children—courtesy of Phil. We'll set up, stay here until the weekend, and make a couple nights of it then.

"One of the children was destroyed. Phil turned a corner too fast and he hadn't made any attempt at proper packing. Celeste's jar fell over and her head came off."

Bill remembered that Celeste had been a female baby with a vagina, a pecker, and a swollen head.

"I ended up burying her beside the road. Ever since her birth, and simultaneous death, she has been in that jar. And not long after, on the road. All these years, on the road. I thought it appropriate she was buried by the highway."

Bill thought probably about a half hour later some dog had dug her up and was making a meal of her in a thicket somewhere.

"Anyway, the whirligig is ours, it'll be here tomorrow. Phil is shipping it in."

There wasn't exactly a murmur of enthusiasm. Setting up that whirligig was a pain in the ass. Even Conrad, who could be easygoing about most things, had said one day he'd rather drink a bucket of runny rat shit than help put that bolt-rattling sonofabitch up.

Usually, it came time for putting together the whirligig, Phil got drunk to do it and called for volunteers to help. It was then that the carnivalites began to suffer minor ailments. Anything from a paper cut to a bad back surfaced. But somehow, every time they camped, the damn thing got put up so unsuspecting folks could risk their lives.

Bill wished Phil had just gone off with his whirligig and not stolen anything. Everyone would have been a lot happier. Now, with that damn whirligig coming back, Bill thought he'd like to hunt Phil down with a pack of dogs, a rifle, and a few angry peasants with torches.

"Who says he'll show?" asked Conrad.

"Well, I had him write out what he'd done on a piece of paper, and I said he didn't show in the morning, I'd give the paper to the cops. Now, I understand a number of you had some trouble yesterday. I'm glad no one was hurt. I was rude earlier today, and I hope Bill and Conrad can forgive me for my loss of temper, and my seeming lack of interest in the living. I assure you, I care about all of you, very much."

"We gonna eat now?" Double Buckwheat asked.

Frost smiled. "I suppose so."

Night settled in, gray at first with strands of the sun ripped up and strewn through it, like orange confetti. Bill, who had been interested in the dark cloud that had settled over them, looked up. It was no longer distinguishable, it was just part of the starless night, like a sack had been pulled over everything.

Everyone went off to their spot to eat. Bill wished it were breakfast, when they ate together at the picnic tables. He felt lonely going back to the Ice Man's trailer. Lonely and confused. He hadn't had such an unsettling day since his mother died. Well, since the firecracker stand robbery. Well, since Deputy Cocksucker and the discovery of the freak show and carnival.

Come to think of it, lately most of his days were unsettling. But today was unsettling in a different way. He wasn't sure if it had been a good day or a bad one. He felt he had truly become friends with Conrad, and he liked the feeling. He had never had a real friend before, just people he could do small crimes with.

147

And Gidget. Jesus, she was something. And there was that stuff about James Dean. He had to see one of his movies sometime. He had to find out more about him, now that he knew he and the Sausage Man weren't one and the same.

And there were other feelings. Guilt feelings. He had betrayed Frost, one of the first people in his life to truly do something for him out of the goodness of his heart. Before, he had seen Frost as a sucker, now he wasn't so sure. Things inside him were being stirred he didn't even know he had.

Twenty-three

Serious rain was thumping down and the river outside sounded as if it were running through the Ice Man's trailer.

Bill was eating a mustard-dipped corn dog he'd warmed in the trailer's little microwave. He was eating it and pondering about the Ice Man being not only frozen, but petrified. Was he petrified because he was frozen, or was he petrified and then frozen, and what was the point of freezing him if he was petrified?

Bill was working these mysteries about in the great room of his head when there was a scratching at the door, like a cat wanting in. At first he thought it might be coming from inside the freezer itself, made by the nails of a petrified hand. He jerked when he heard it and dropped the corn dog. It rolled across the glass and stopped, smearing mustard so that it looked like a great bug collision on a windshield.

Glancing at the Ice Man, he discovered the old boy hadn't moved a smidgen. The scratching was coming from the door and it made the hairs on his upper back and neck salute. He was suddenly brought to mind of all those cats of his mother's he had bagged and drowned. He had a vision of the raging river having washed them free and brought them back to seek him out.

Bill went over to the door, put his ear to it, heard Gidget's voice say, "Bill?"

When he opened the door she was dressed in a yellow rain slicker with a hood. She looked like a plastic monk. He let her in and she took off the raincoat immediately and tossed it on the floor. Water ran out from under it. She said, "I thought you weren't ever going to open the door."

"I didn't hear you out there at first. Or I didn't know what it was."

"I'm soaked to the bone. Damn water ran inside the slicker. It's blowing ass over tea kettle."

Gidget was wearing blue jean shorts and a man's white T-shirt. Her shirt was wet and her breasts were visible through it.

"I don't know you should be here."

"Hell, Frost is out. I slipped him a Mickey. He won't wake up until tomorrow morning. I said I was going to fix us drinks, and I did, but mine didn't have a Mickey in it."

"Someone could have seen you come over here."

"In this rain, not likely. I couldn't see myself out there. I damn near wandered off the edge into the river. It's really perfect for me coming here."

"Why are you here?"

Gidget looked at Bill as if she had just discovered his head had been hollowed out with a spoon. "Didn't today mean anything to you?"

150

"I wasn't sure it meant much to you. Way you disappeared."

"I guess I was thinking, Bill. I was kind of overwhelmed. I was thinking about us. I was thinking about lots of things. For Christ sakes, offer me a towel. You got any liquor?"

Bill shook his head and got a towel. By the time he handed it to her she was out of her shorts, shirt, and shoes, and was wiping off. She wore only black panties with frilly black lace on the edges. When she spread her legs to wipe the insides of her thighs, he discovered the panties were split in the middle; the split rolled on either side of her pubic mound.

"Those made like that?"

Gidget, who seemed unaware of the fact she was nearly naked, glanced up. "Oh, yeah. They come like that. You like 'em?"

"Yeah."

"Come here, baby."

He moved toward her. When he touched her, her skin was cool and clammy, but after a few moments it was warm and damp. He touched her everywhere he could. Her lips were soft and her tongue was like a hot probe.

Finally he pushed her away and came out of his clothes. She did not help him undress. She bent across the freezer, her naked breasts against the mustard.and the glass, her tail, trimmed by black lace, lifted to him.

Bill did not remember moving across the room to take her from behind. He felt as if he had fallen into her from a great height. He began to thrust. She moaned and her breasts slid across the mustard-smeared glass and made a sound like a squeegee cleaning a windshield. The corn dog bobbed about and leaped to the floor and rolled under the bed.

"Hurt me," she said, and he slapped her buttocks with his hands, leaving great red palm and finger marks. He was reminded of pictures he had seen of Indian ponies where their owners had dipped hands in red paint and pressed their palms against the horse's sides, leaving bright signs of ownership and decoration.

He spanked her harder and rammed her harder and she let out little happy hurt sounds. She rose up on the balls of her feet and her ass grew firmer and he bored deeper, trying not to finish too soon. He thought of other things to hold it back. He looked at the Ice Man through smears of mustard, for the heat of their activity had warmed the glass and made him visible.

Sweat filled Bill's eyes as he continued to work. He grabbed Gidget's hair and she squealed. He pulled her head back and kissed the side of her throat, feeling her pulse throb against his lips. He rubbed the mustard all over her.

"I can't wait," he said. "Jeez . . . I'm gonna finish."

"Now?"

"Oh, Jesus."

"It's okay, baby. Give me all of it."

He jerked her panties with his hands and they tore away. He tossed them on the floor and thrust into her hard, and just as he was about to let loose Gidget slipped from him, dropped and turned and took him in her mouth and he let go.

He pulled her up and lay her on her back across the glass and got between her legs, worked his tongue while he reached up and squeezed her nipples. Seconds later she let go with a soft scream. They found their way to the shower and bathed together, and made love standing up, then they dried off and lay down in bed.

"Won't he wake up and miss you?"

"He won't wake up till morning. I've used that stuff before. Thing I hate is he'll wake up at all."

"You shouldn't talk like that."

"Shouldn't I?"

"No, you shouldn't."

"I don't think I knew how bad I wanted to go away from here until you showed."

"You didn't like me, remember?"

"I didn't like that face. When you cleared up I liked you fine. You look like James Dean."

"Aren't we supposed to like each other for who we are?"

"Bullshit. I want someone looks good and wants me as bad as I want him. Let me tell you something, Frost don't look that good naked. And he has this kind of smell. I can't describe it. It's not a bad smell. He's always pure and clean. It's like . . . I don't know. Do you smell us?"

"Yeah."

"Hot and nasty and I like it. He's like angel food cake out of the oven, all sweet and fresh baked. It gets to me. And that hand. I make him wear a glove when we fuck."

Bill thought of the time Frost had stopped the fight between Conrad and Phil. He had been wearing the glove then. He remembered Gidget at the door of the motor home, somewhat peeved and slightly dressed.

"Why the glove?"

"I don't like looking at it."

"You still have to look at it, except it's in a glove."

"Yeah, but I don't have to feel that hand. When he lays against me, I feel that hand. If he lifts up, the hand drops and touches me . . . You just don't know. That hand . . .

Sometimes I think it's alive, not just flapping around against me. I keep thinking that hand wants to get hold of my throat."

"Frost don't seem that way to me."

"He isn't, but I think that hand is . . . and don't smile at me like that. You've never had to touch it. It's like something wet and muddy crawling over you. It feels like you think a snake ought to feel. I can't take much more of it. He's talking about us having a baby, and I'm thinking, yeah, great, we have a baby I can teach it to wash three hands. It might have four. It could work here in the carnival, wave at the crowd and knit a sweater. I don't want to have no freak baby. It's bad enough I got to have a freak inside me trying to get off."

"But you went with him. It was your choice."

"I'd have screwed a monkey while I was blowin' the organ grinder to get out of that damn restaurant. I didn't know what I was gettin' into. I thought I could take it. I can't take it. I want you, not him. We're a beautiful couple, Bill."

Bill's body turned cool and goose bumps rose over him and the bumps were hard, like headstones. No one had ever wanted him before, least of all someone who looked like, felt like, and smelled like Gidget.

"I got to get rid of him, you know."

"We could go away."

"I thought about that."

"We could just go off and you could get a divorce."

"I could, yeah."

"It seems like the only way."

"I've gone off before, and I'm always just the same when I get to where I go. I might as well have stayed before I went. Everything I do is like fuckin' déjà vu. This time I got to do different."

"We could go off and you could get a divorce and I could get a job."

"Doing what? Brain surgery? You look good, baby, and I like what you do to me, how you make me feel, but you're not exactly a hot job property."

"It wouldn't matter as long as we had each other."

"It would matter to me. I don't want to live in no shit-hole little town in a goddamn trailer with three snot-nosed brats pulling at my dress. I may not be worth a shit, and you may not be either, but I still want something better."

"Then what can we do?"

"How much do you love me?"

Love hadn't been mentioned before. Bill was taken aback. "I . . . I don't know."

Gidget turned away from him and stuck her face in a pillow and began to cry. "Jesus. Fuckin' Jesus."

"What?"

"Here I am pouring my heart out to you, and I'm just a piece to you. You don't care about me. You don't care I got to stay with this freak. It don't mean a thing to you."

"I didn't say that."

Gidget got up, still crying. She found her panties in the light from the lamp and tried to pull them on, but they were wrecked. She threw them on the floor, began to thrash about looking for the rest of her clothes.

Bill lay on the bed and looked at her and tried to think of something to say.

"I thought you loved me," she said as she pulled her shorts on one leg.

"I didn't say I didn't love you."

"It's not something you have to think about, god-damnit."

"Look, Gidget. I love you. I just . . . I've never been in love before. I didn't know how to say it."

She smiled and sniffed. "You just say it. That's all. You just say it."

"I love you."

She pulled her shorts off the one leg she had managed to get them on, came back to bed and rolled up against him and ran her fingers down his cheeks and kissed him. They lay together for a while, not speaking. Bill broke the ice.

"So what do we do?"

"You want to be together, right?"

"I said so."

"Then we do what we have to do."

Bill let that one roll around inside his thoughts for a while. "God in heaven, Gidget. We couldn't do that."

"We could."

"We shouldn't. I mean, I've done some things, but I haven't ever done anything like that. Well, not exactly."

"What do you mean not exactly?"

He told her about his mother, the firecracker stand robbery and how his partner had shot the operator. He told her everything. It came out like water boiling over, every little detail.

"That stand operator should have kept his mouth shut and just given the money. That fella Chaplin didn't do any more than he had to do. It just didn't work out in the long run, but he was doing what needed to be done. The cop you didn't kill, he killed himself. You haven't killed anybody and you're whining."

"I'm not whinin'. I'm just sayin'."

"Sounds like a whine to me."

Bill lay still. "I planned the whole thing, but I didn't mean for nothing like that. It's one thing for a murder to happen, it's another to plot it and do it yourself. And the truth is, I like Frost. I owe him."

"Maybe you do, but you've paid that debt. It's not like a lifetime thing."

"There's a line I've stepped over already and I don't like it. I do this on purpose, there ain't even a line. We shouldn't do something like that."

"Maybe we shouldn't, but we could, and I would. And there isn't any line, Bill. Never has been. The only line is the one you draw yourself. Listen here, hon. I got to get loose, and I divorce him, I got nothing. He dies, a little accident, I got a little something. And I got you. And you got those checks of your mother's. I'm a forger, remember. It would be seed money for us to get going, you know."

"You said he dies you got a little something. What little something?"

"The Ice Man. The carnival, for that matter. Do you know how much that Ice Man takes in? It isn't exactly Fort Knox numbers, but you could live pretty good. Get rid of the rest of these freaks, ditch 'em. Just keep the Ice Man, take him around."

"Wouldn't you make more with the carnival altogether?"

"Sure. Shit, Bill, I don't care. I'm just saying we get rid of Frost, we got the Ice Man, carnival if we want it, and we got your mother's checks. It's a good start. Time comes we want to sell the Ice Man, we get a good price, and we use that money to invest in something else."

"Something straight."

"Yeah. I don't want to run the Ice Man around Texas all my life. I just want to get shed of Frost and have some seed money, a little income till we get our shit together. We could maybe open some cafe or something, hire waitresses to do what I used to do. I don't even care you pinch one or two of them on the ass once in a while."

Bill grinned. "We could do that, couldn't we?"

"Or something like it."

"I don't know. Frost has done me all right."

"Good. Take advantage of it. Build on that. Look at it this way, Bill, an opportunity is an opportunity, and if it comes to you, you ought to take it. You don't look to me you're a fella with a lot of grabs at brass rings."

"Could be there's a warrant out on me. You think about that? You and me doing this thing, then going into something like that, them looking for me. He dies, cops'll be around asking questions."

"We'll dodge it until it blows over. Hell, cops don't catch one in ten criminals anymore, and I bet there's not that many people sweating over a firecracker stand and its owner. Then again, there may not be any warrants. Probably don't even know you're involved. We start with this one thing, then we worry about the other problems as we come to them."

"Christ, I don't know."

"Tell you what," Gidget said, getting up, sliding into her shorts more easily this time. "You think about the poontang you aren't getting and the poontang he's getting, and you think about that dead hand of his rubbing me down." She fastened her shorts and pulled on her T-shirt. "You think about that, baby. Then you let me know how you feel. Tell me you haven't got anything against him. Fact he's fuckin' me like I was a fertility goddess ought to be cause enough you want to see him dead. What he's getting, you aren't getting. Remember that."

Gidget pulled the slicker over her head, stopped at the

door, and looked back. "You ought to clean up that mustard. And there's a corn dog under your bed. I can see it from here."

She went out in the rain and closed the door. After a time, Bill got up, cleaned the freezer, rinsed off the corn dog, rewarmed it in the microwave and ate it.

Twenty-four

Next day the rain cleared up. Dampness hung from every tree limb and leaf and blade of grass and the trailers were slicked as if coated with gloss. The whirligig arrived from its last location via the trailer, along with the Pickled Punks. Phil had driven the trailer himself and a wetback he'd hired followed him in a car with a smoking exhaust. It looked like an old-fashioned mosquito fogger.

Phil and Frost parleyed and Phil went out of there with a scowl on his face, his South of the Border driver at the wheel.

Frost rounded up enough folks to erect the whirligig. It was wet from being dragged around on the damp grass. Much of it had worn bright silver through the green paint.

This was the very thing that was getting Frost. The green paint worn away. He was standing under the whirligig with the only two helpers who hadn't faded. Double Buckwheat and Conrad, who, as usual, was smoking a cigarette. Breakfast had not only involved eggs but grits, so Double Buckwheat's two heads looked like Brillo pads that had scoured most of the breakfast dishes of the continental United States.

Each stood with a hand over his eyes to shield out the brightness of the sun. Conrad had on a felt hat with a black band with a feather in it. He looked kind of cute, the way a dog does when you dress it up in clothes.

Bill, who had not participated in erecting the whirligig or done anything else this morning, came out and leaned against the Ice Man's trailer, eating a corn dog. He watched them stare up at the whirligig. He would have felt last night had been a dream had he not woken up this morning and found Gidget's ruined panties. He had lain in bed with them over his face, his nose sticking through the slit designed for what he felt might be the best part of her. He smelled the panties for a time, and when he got up, he realized he had missed breakfast.

He ate the corn dog slowly. He was so worn out his teeth hurt. He thought about what he and Gidget had talked about, and decided maybe Gidget had been half goofy last night, thinking out loud about something she didn't really want.

He walked over to where Frost, Double Buckwheat, and Conrad stood looking up at the whirligig.

"Bird watching?" Bill asked.

"Bird watching," one of Double Buckwheat's heads said.

"Needs paint," Frost said.

"Needs paint," the other Double Buckwheat head said.

"I think it's all right," Conrad said. "Especially since he's wanting to get us up there to paint it. This ground down here would be littered with pinheads and such. And I'm not so good at climbing either."

"Not everyone here is mentally handicapped," Frost said.

"Handicapped," Double Buckwheat said.

"Let me think on that," Conrad said. "I ain't so sure."

"He ain't sure," the other head said.

"I'm just saying it needs paint," Frost said.

"Paint," said Double Buckwheat.

"I know how you are when you think something needs paint," Conrad said. "Or something needs this, or something needs that. You can't leave it alone until it's done. And that generally means I'm in on the doing it."

"You do work here, Conrad."

"I do everything but wipe the twins' ass," Conrad said, "and I ain't about to add to my job description ass-wiping or climbing up there on that bolt-rattling sonofabitch to paint it."

"Sonofabitch," both heads said. .

"Very well," Frost said. "I'll paint it myself."

"He'll paint it," one head said.

"It's gonna rain again anyhow," Conrad said.

"Rain," the other head said.

Frost turned and looked at Double Buckwheat. He smiled. "Do you think you boys could go somewhere else to stand? And maybe you could wash your hair."

One of the Buckwheats said, "Packin' it in," and off they went.

"I think the rain is finished for the next day or two," Frost said, "and if I can get it painted, the sun's hot enough it'll dry out all right before this weekend's show."

"What makes you think the rain is over with?" Conrad said.

"It's stopped."

"Oh, good. You're a regular weatherman."

"What makes you think it'll continue? Huh?"

"Hey, you win. Just as long as I don't paint it." Conrad peeled back his ugly lips, showed his teeth, tipped his hat, and went off on all fours.

"What do you think, Bill?"

"Mr. Frost, I ain't got a clue."

"Would you help me paint it?"

It wasn't something Bill looked forward to, but he felt he was in no position to quarrel.

"Sure."

Frost went into town and came back with lots of green paint and a sackful of brushes. By midday the dampness had burned off and the whirligig was dry and receptive to paint.

Frost enlisted the help of a couple of others but as the day progressed, like vapor, they disappeared, leaving brushes and cans in whirligig buckets. Complaints of old ailments kept popping up. One of the workers, whose only handicap was his lack of hygiene, was not missed. There had been just enough wind up there to blow his armpit aroma about, and by the time the man climbed down with some minor excuse, Bill and Frost were glad to see him go. Bill felt as if he had been wrestling a stink demon all day, and was about worn out from it.

Even though a certain amount of climbing was to be expected, mostly they rode about on the rails and in the cars by having one of the pinheads pull the switch. The problem was making the pinhead not pull the switch, and after half a day the pinhead wandered off and was last seen rubbing his ass out by the river.

Bill climbed down and tried to work the switch, but nothing happened. He had to go get Conrad to take a look. Conrad sniffed about and worked this and worked that. He got a little box of tools and tore off the gearbox lid and eyeballed the situation. The gearbox was packed with dirt. It was surprising it had worked as long as it had. Phil had left one last little surprise for Frost.

"It's screwed," Conrad yelled up. "Phil packed the gearbox with dirt."

Bill glanced up. He could make out Frost looking over the edge of the stranded bucket he was in. Frost let out a sigh audible all over the camp.

"It won't run at all?" he yelled down.

"Nope," Conrad said.

"Can it be fixed?"

"It can be replaced."

Another sigh from Frost. "I guess the only thing is to climb around and finish what we can reach. We've gone this far. Tomorrow I'll go into town and see I can find someone who can fix or jury-rig a new gearbox. Phil had some problems, but I wouldn't have expected this of him."

"Hell, I would have expected worse," Conrad said. "He was hoping it would jam up carnival night, kill some major revenue."

"Bill," Frost yelled down. "Do you think you could climb up here and help me finish this top railing, and the last few buckets?"

Bill didn't much like the idea, but he nodded.

"If you fall," Conrad said with a smile, "tuck your chin and think rubber."

"Yeah, right."

Conrad slapped Bill on the thigh and four-pawed it back to U.S. Grant's trailer.

Bill took off his paint-splattered shirt and started up. It took him about fifteen minutes to get up to the bucket next to Frost.

"Thanks, Billy Boy. It's good to see you're true-blue."

"Sure," Bill said, picked up a brush and began to paint the railing that held the buckets. The sun was hot. It felt good for a while, but after a time he began to burn and his wrists ached from working the brush. He had paint all over him and no shirt to put on to keep out the sun.

Once he looked down, and there, with her hands over her eyes, wearing a soft cotton dress with pink and blue flowers on it, was Gidget. The dress was gathered around her and fit like a condom. You could see every outline of her there was to see. A pinhead came up behind her and lifted her dress from behind.

Like it was nothing new, Gidget whipped out her right hand and beaned the pinhead across the nose. The pinhead wandered off holding his snout.

Frost smiled and waved at her. She waved back.

As it grew dark, about suppertime, the sun fell through the metal of the whirligig and filled the bucket where Bill stood with melted caramel light. Frost turned and smiled. In that moment, to Bill, he seemed of another world. The dissolving sunlight had made him golden.

"I'm pooped," Frost said.

"Yeah."

"I think we should seal up the paint, have some supper. Finish up in the morning. Tomorrow, we can do the last bits as we climb down. It'll be a little tricky, but we're careful, tie the buckets to out belts, we can do it. But we'll do it tomorrow. I've had it with the smell of paint."

"Might be easier to just get the gearbox fixed first, don't you think?"

"It might be, but I like to finish what I start. We can be through in an hour or two if we start early, and I'll go into town then and see about a mechanic of some kind. You got much paint left?"

"No. Practically out."

"Yeah. Me too."

They climbed down.

About a half hour later, Bill was fresh out of the shower, having gotten all the paint off himself, and the stench of it out of his nostrils. There was a knock on the door. Bill wrapped a towel around his waist and answered it. It was Frost.

"Look here, son. I need a favor."

"Come in."

"No. I'll make it quick. I'm tuckered out and to be honest there's something I want to see on the television. But I'll give you some money for paint, and a little extra for yourself. I want you to run into town. They got a Wal-Mart there, which is about all that's open this time a night. Fact it stays open twenty-four hours. That's where I got the paint. I want you to get some more. I got the name of the paint written down."

Frost produced a strip of paper with the name and paint number on it. "This is what you want. And get the number of gallons written on here."

"All right."

"Oh, I'm sending Gidget with you. She knows where the Wal-Mart is."

"Sure."

166

"She wants it, stop by and buy her a little something to eat afterwards."

"Sure."

Frost gave Bill some money. After he left, Bill dressed and put the slip of paper in his pocket. He worked his hair in the bathroom a while, trying to comb it more like the picture of James Dean. He went outside. Gidget, still dressed in the white dress with flowers on it, was leaning beside Frost's car smoking a cigarette. She didn't show any happiness in seeing him.

She produced the car keys and Bill took the driver's side and she sat in her place with the window down, flicking ashes out. She looked as if she'd rather be taking a car aerial enema than going to town with him.

When they were about three miles down the road, Bill glanced at her out of the corner of his eye. She smiled, slid over next to him and kissed his neck.

"I had to play it that way, baby. I couldn't look too excited."

"Sure. No problem."

"Man, you look good all browned from the sun."

"It's more like burned."

"Listen, hon, you know what Frost is going to do? He's going to get up early and take the paint and finish before you get up. He thinks it's some kind of surprise. So he'll be up there before you get up, see. You'll be in bed, and I'll be in the motor home, and he's up there in that rickety old whirligig. Everyone has tried to make him get rid of it. It's old and it's coming apart. It's dangerous."

"I don't like where this is going."

"I think you'll like where it ends up. Tonight, when we get back, you wait until late, then you take a flashlight and climb up there and loosen the bolts in the bucket where he'll start painting tomorrow. Loosen them and set it such a way a little movement will make it tip. Since where ya'll quit today is at the top . . . Well, it's quite a drop. He's a big man."

Bill had a good grip on the wheel. They went out of darkness and into the beginnings of light from the town.

"Turn here," Gidget said.

They went down a long street and came to a highway and Gidget had Bill turn right. He went along there and past some houses and came to the Wal-Mart on the right. He pulled up in the huge lot way away from the store. So far out they would have to walk a distance to go inside. He cut the engine and sat.

"You've drugged him, made him sleep. Why not just do it that way? Too many pills. Why's it got to be done like this?"

"It's got to look like an accident. We can't be around. I drugged him, they got tests will show that. They'd find out right away. This is better."

"Something like this, it can't be undone," Bill said. "I know. I got some things I'd like to undo. It always seems easy, but it's more than you see. I don't know nothin', but I know that."

"Yeah. Well I know this. I want you. I like the way you look. I like that eight inches of dick you got. And I don't want to scrape for three years or four or five or the rest of my life. I need some kind of start. We deserve it."

"Do we?"

"You deserve what you think you deserve. You get what you get, and sometimes, you have to go get it. You understand?"

"You really think it'll work?"

"He wants to do something nice for you. He thinks you're swell."

"Oh shit . . ."

"Just listen. You worked all day when everyone else took off. He appreciates that. He's going to climb up there to-morrow right at sunrise and finish. He wants it done so it's got time to dry and he can get into town to have someone fix the gearbox. He gets in that whirligig bucket, starts moving his big ass around . . . he's dumped. It'll look like an accident. No one will know."

"How am I gonna loosen the bolt?"

"With one of his wrenches. I got it out of his toolbox. It's hid outside the motor home now, but I haven't been able to get it over to your trailer. We bring the paint back, I'll give you the wrench."

"Conrad sleeps on top of the motor home sometimes."

"Not since he's been sticking his dick in Synora."

"Synora?"

"The bearded lady."

"Oh." Bill felt bad he didn't even know the bearded lady's name. Conrad was his friend, and he hadn't even bothered to know his woman's name.

"You got to learn to pay attention to details, baby. That little thing with Phil, it's put Conrad in regular with her. He sleeps in her place. And the weather has been unpre-dictable. Think about it."

"I'm thinking."

"You can get up there quick and easy and undo the bolt and climb down. Take the wrench, wipe off any prints might be on it, and throw it in the river. That way, there's paint inside it or rust from the bolt, they can't trace it, and even if you miss a fingerprint, it isn't going to hold under-water. And them finding it in the river there, I doubt it.

Not the way it's churning. Toss it in there and it's gone for-ever. It's just an accident."

"But it isn't."

"In a day or two, far as I'm concerned, it's an accident."

"The cops will come around. They'll talk to all of us, and I may be wanted for that firecracker stand thing."

"Cops come, you don't need to even come out unless they ask to see everyone. It'll just be a dumb accident. Let me tell you something, a thing happens at the carnival no-body busts their ass to find out about it. No one is all that worried about a bunch of freaks. I know I'm not. Let's get the paint."

Twenty-five

They bought the paint and Gidget made it a point not to stand too close to Bill or to look in any way interested in him while they got it and went through the checkout line.

They left there, and on their way home she asked him if he was supposed to buy her something.

"Frost said if you want it."

"I don't want it, but if I did, it'd be about ten dollars' worth. Give me the ten dollars."

Bill worked his wallet out and put it on the seat. She took ten, and then a five.

"Say I'm real hungry. I think I should get what you would have spent, don't you?"

"I guess."

They drove on and Gidget had him pull down a little clay road and onto a trail that wound up a hill into a clutch of trees overlooking the road below through pine limbs. The road and trail were muddy from all the rain and Bill feared they'd get stuck, but they forged on, sliding a bit, and finally they came to rest at the peak of the hill. Gidget lit up a cigarette and looked out the open window. She spent a few minutes doing that, neither of them talking.

"Years ago, when I was in high school, I used to park with a boyfriend up here. He was a smart, neat guy. Good-looking enough. He wanted to go to college and take care of me and he thought I had some art talent. He thought I could do something with it. I wasn't patient enough. He went on and did well. Me, I'm still out here."

"What about me, baby?"

"You're something, hon. I like the way you look. You're kind of cheap and not too smart and probably rotten to the core, just like me. We deserve one another."

Bill tried to decide if that was a compliment. While he was contemplating, Gidget hiked up her dress with one hand while she smoked with the other, and showed him she didn't have on panties. She lay back on the seat and threw one leg on the dash and took another hit off her smoke.

"You haven't got time to get fancy, and you don't need to make me come, but I figured you'd probably want a little of this. Sooie, honey! Come and get it."

Bill unbuckled his pants and pushed them and his underwear down to his knees and showed her that he did indeed want a little of it. He felt a little ashamed to just jump on her, but not so proud he didn't do it. She smoked with one hand and stroked the back of his head with the other. Once when he looked up, her eyes were half closed and smoke was rolling out of her nostrils, and he assumed, somewhat painfully, that she was thinking of the college boy she didn't marry. He made sure that with every stroke he hurt her a little.

Five minutes later he finished and she lit up a fresh cigarette. Five minutes after that the car was churning through
sticky mud, but they made it, got back on the road and slid
around there until they reached the highway.

Bill said, "I feel kinda guilty, just knocking off a piece
like that. Not doing anything for you."

"Hey, it felt all right. We didn't have time for nothing
else. I wanted you to remember what it is you're gonna be
gettin' regular-like when Frost is dead."

Bill sighed.

"It'll be all right. Listen here. You love me?"

"Yes."

"More than anything?"

"Sure."

"Then there isn't any holdup, is there?"

Bill didn't answer.

When they got back to the carnival Conrad was outside,
smoking a cigarette, looking at the stars. He watched Bill
and Gidget carefully. Gidget got out of the car and nodded
at Conrad and went inside the motor home. Bill thought
about the wrench a moment, then went over and stood by
Conrad, bummed a smoke. Conrad lit him up.

"So," said Conrad, "you've taken up smoking?"

"I used to smoke my Mom's cigarettes. But just when I
was nervous."

"You're nervous?"

"Not really. I don't know. I guess."

"About what?"

"Life."

"You stayin' out of ditches?"

"Sure."

"I mean little ditches with hair round the edges."

"Sure. Old man just sent us into town for paint, that's all. How's it with Synora?"

"U.S. Grant? Hell, no one really calls her Synora. She's talking about shaving her beard, though. Then maybe that's what she ought to be called. She's lost some pounds lately, thinking about going straight and looking good. Me, I guess I'm stuck this way or no way."

"She not going to stay with the carnival?"

"I don't know. I seen this special on TV the other night. It was on carny folks, about how all of 'em really love the life. Let me tell you, from my viewpoint the life sucks. If she can leave the carnival, go straight, I was her, I'd do it. She could maybe even get that electrolysis, or whatever it is that removes hair permanently."

"That'd be all right, I reckon."

"What I figure, she leaves, well, that's it for me. Unless she wants to keep a dog in the suburbs. You know, buy me a little doggie bowl, take me for walks. She leaves here, she's got some kind of degree she earned by correspondence. She don't have to do this. Me, I not only don't have a degree, I look like a goddamn dog."

"But a very nice dog."

Conrad laughed.

"It'll work out."

"Yeah," Conrad said, dropping his cigarette butt on the ground, grinding it with the leather band on his hand. "It'll work out all right, but I may not like how it works."

Conrad looked up at the whirligig. The starlight made the paint shine, though you couldn't really tell anything about the color.

"I got to give it to Frost," Conrad said. "Damn thing does look better. Least in the dark."

"We didn't finish," Bill said. "We got to do that tomor-row. Up there at the top we got places to paint."

"Yeah, well, I should have got up there and helped him, I guess. I was pretty hard-ass. Actually, I'm quite a climber, I just don't want him to know it. So I lied."

"It don't matter. Tomorrow morning we'll finish. I'm dreading the shit out of it, but we'll get it done."

Conrad pulled back his rubbery lips and showed his teeth. There were bits of tobacco in them.

"Bill, you know, you're all right."

"Thanks. You ain't so bad yourself."

"You fish much?"

"Used to, some."

"That river out there calms down tomorrow, we ought to drop a line in there. Whatdaya say?"

"It's something to think about."

"I got the tackle."

"Well, all right."

"Good. Me, I'm going to see if I can catch a program on the television, then see if I can get lucky with Synora."

"Yeah, well be careful doing that. You'll get stinky on your dinky."

"One can hope."

Twenty-six

In the Ice Man's trailer, late at night, early morning actually, Bill sat on the stool where Frost sat when he lectured about the Ice Man. With eyes closed, the hair dryer in his hand, held between his legs limply, Bill went over the spiel Frost gave, imagined himself giving the talk while wearing a suit the color of vanilla ice cream, a peach-colored shirt, and a dark blue tie. He imagined two-tone shoes, white and brown, polished to the point of being blinding.

He imagined a crowd around the freezer, hanging on his every word. All the women in the crowd were as pretty as Gidget, but not so fire-kissed. The women were looking down at the Ice Man, sneaking looks at the old man's privates, glancing now and then at Bill as he talked with authority. All of the women wanted him. Bill was certain of that much. It was in their eyes. They wanted Bill because the Ice Man, a dead messenger from the past, had heated them up, sending out sensuality from beyond death, frost, and petrification.

He wanted them too, and would give each their turn, and the men would not care, because they knew, absolutely knew, he deserved it and that for him to have their women was an honor.

Bill opened his eyes and gazed down at the glass. It was frosted. He slowly lifted the hair dryer between his legs and struck the button. The dryer roared and gave a burst of hot air, heated the glass, and caused the frost to dissipate.

When he stared down at the Ice Man—appearing suddenly as if rising out of a block of ice—Bill experienced a sensation of dropping inside the freezer and entering into the Ice Man and looking up and out of his eyes. Above him was the water-beaded glass, and through it he could see his face looking down with hollow eyes and through his empty sockets he could see his empty universe. No stars. No moon. No form. Just void.

It was such a disconcerting feeling Bill had to close his eyes so that he could neither see what he saw or what he thought he saw. He wondered what was going on inside him.

Until Frost, Bill had felt there was just him as he was. There were no sides to it. Good and Bad weren't real to him. They were words. Now he felt he had seen some light and had liked it. Frost had shone the light on him. Frost had believed in him. And now he had a friend, Conrad, and the light was brighter yet.

Then along came Gidget, dragging shadow, looking like, tasting like, some calorie-filled confection, and he had tasted her, and he had felt as Adam must have felt when he bit into the apple. Light going out. Dirt giving way beneath his feet, grabbing at roots and vines that wouldn't hold.

Bill took a deep breath. He told himself he had to hang on, had to poke his shoes into the dirt and make toeholds. Had to climb up and out and into the light. Had to not do this thing Gidget wanted. Had to stay out of that ditch Conrad warned him about. Only Conrad was wrong, it wasn't a ditch. It was a crevasse.

The hair dryer droned on. Bill tried to find a spot for himself behind the sound, some place to hide, but he couldn't. His misery was larger and louder than sound. He opened his eyes again and looked at the Ice Man.

All you got to do is not do it, he thought.

All you got to do is leave it be.

You haven't got the wrench, weren't able to get it, so you can't do it anyway, so you don't have to do a thing.

You don't have to touch that woman again. Nothing makes you do it but yourself, and you are the captain of yourself.

Let it pass and you'll be okay.

There was a knock on the door. Bill jerked, the dryer came unplugged. The burst of heat went away and the dryer fell limp in his hand.

The night air was cool because of the river. The air tasted like the river and the damp East Texas soil. It was a fresh sweet smell that he imagined was not too unlike that of being born.

On the steps of his trailer he saw the wrench. He looked toward the motor home. There went Gidget, moving fast, her buttocks working underneath her cotton dress as if one were wrestling with the other. She went inside the motor home and quietly closed the door without so much as looking back.

Bill stared at the wrench for a full minute. Then he bent over and picked it up. It was heavy. Gidget's smell was on it. He was the captain, but his ship was on the reef.

Twenty-seven

He had the wrench in his belt as he started his climb. He went up carefully. There was a nightsweat dampness on the metal and it was hard to get a hand or foothold, and the fresh paint had dried smooth and that made it even harder.

The sky had cleared. As he climbed, he nearly lost himself in the stars above. They were thick and beautiful. There was a crescent moon. It was like a single cat eye, partially open, waiting for a mouse. Crickets chirped and great frogs sang bass out on the river. The pines seemed to have gathered the moon's light like a mist and they had the appearance of narrow pyramids stacked close together.

Twice the wrench in his belt clanged against the metal, and he looked over his shoulder, but saw no one. As he reached the uppermost bucket he heard a sound below. Looking down, he saw it was one of the pinheads and Double Buckwheat. They had come out of nowhere.

180

Bill stood still, one foot about to step into the bucket. He saw the pinhead was the one they called Peter. He could tell because Peter had a brilliant pink head with a ring of hair on it like a dirty bird's nest. Pete and Double Buckwheat were talking. Pete was sayin', "No. Uh uh," which was about a third of his vocabulary.

"Then it's you," said one of the Buckwheats. "Us first, then you."

"Uh uh. No."

"We trade," said the other Buckwheat.

"No."

"Two heads better than one."

Pete paused at this. He paused for a long time. Double Buckwheat handed him what looked like a wrapped candy bar. Pete might have said something, Bill couldn't be sure. Pete turned and went between two trailers and a moment later Double Buckwheat followed. Bill eased into the bucket, crouched down and peeked over the edge.

He watched Double Buckwheat and Pete move like ghosts through the night, one pale with a head you could toss rings on, the other a double-headed black ghost. They disappeared into a copse of woods near the river.

Bill decided they were far enough away, and he had to go on and do it, because somehow he didn't know how not to do it. Watching Gidget's buttocks pound one another had battered down his resistance. Those buttocks banged like cannons in his brain.

He took the wrench from his belt and felt around for the bolts. When he found one, he took a deep breath and sat still until his eyes adjusted to the interior of the bucket. Then he took the wrench and turned the nut on the bolt until it could be plucked off with the fingers. With that one done, he slid over and unfastened another. The bucket creaked a little.

Bill thought, now how do I do this and get out of this goddamn bucket without it tipping me? But he kept at it until three bolts were loose. He eased himself to the side and climbed out carefully, leaned over and unfastened the last few bolts so that the nuts, like the others, were hardly on the bolts. A breeze could blow them off. Frost, not knowing they were loose, moving around in there, trying to work, was going to drop.

Bill looked down and saw the fall was a formidable one. If Frost hit the ground he might live, but if he tumbled and dove on his head, or maybe landed hard on his heels or back, he was going to be either dead or severely fucked up. Maybe that was what would happen. He would be paralyzed, but alive, then Gidget would have him to nurse. That would be fitting. But no, that wouldn't do either. One way or another, Gidget would get him. And realizing that, knowing that it was inevitable no matter what he did, Bill slipped the wrench in his belt and climbed down.

He went between trailers and on out to the river's edge trying to find a place that looked deep so he could toss the wrench, and as he walked through a patch of pecan trees, he heard a Double Buckwheat head say, "Yes sir, that's what we need."

Bill dropped to his stomach, lay still and listened. Shit, he had stupidly forgotten about Pete and Double Buckwheat. They had come out of the copse of trees while he was busy and had moved over to stand beneath the handful of old pecan trees on the edge of the river. There was so much on his mind he hadn't remembered they were out here. He had been thinking of throwing the wrench away, and had come all the way out here to do it. He would have been better off tossing it in the river near his trailer. Of all the stupid goddamn things to do. Now here were two, or rather three, witnesses who could say they saw him wandering around at night.

Bill lay there and listened to the river, then behind the noise of the water he heard a sound like a baby sucking air from an empty bottle. Bill crawled forward on the damp ground until he could see Double Buckwheat between two pecan trees. Pete was on his knees in front of him. Pete was sucking Double Buckwheat's dick like it was a straw and there was an apple he wanted on the other side and didn't know it wouldn't come through.

So, that's what the parley and candy bar had been about. Double Buckwheat had been working on the pinhead to blow him . . . Them. Jesus. Did Double Buckwheat have one dick or two?

Bill strained his eyes for a look. One.

After a moment Double Buckwheat jerked, and Pete pulled his head back. Double Buckwheat's black dick flopped up and out and spewed like a little hose full of mayonnaise. Some of what was in Double Buckwheat sprayed Pete and the ground.

"Tastes bad," Pete said.

"Oh," Double Buckwheat said, and put out a hand and held himself up with a pecan tree. "Oh."

Pete stood up and unfastened his pants. "Now me."

"Nope," Double Buckwheat said.

"You said would."

"Nope."

Pete just stood there, his pathetic little pink pecker sticking out like an insect proboscis. "Said would."

"Won't."

Double Buckwheat fastened his pants.

183

Pete tried a backup position. "Pull it?"

Double Buckwheat hauled off and hit Pete a hard one on the side of the jaw with his fist. Pete hit the ground, rolled on his back, his pink pecker lolling limply to one side.

Double Buckwheat, grinning and happy, went away from there and left Pete unconscious. Double Buckwheat walked right by where Bill lay and didn't see him. When he passed, Bill turned and saw the twins heading into camp. He looked back at Pete, still lying quietly.

Bill wondered if this happened on a regular basis. It wasn't like Pete was going to learn from his mistakes. Bill eased up and went between the pecans and pulled the wrench from his belt and tossed it far out into the river. It made a splash and was gone, probably tumbling along the bottom, burying up in river mud, something for a big cat-fish to ponder.

When Bill turned, he saw that Pete was on his feet, hold-ing his jaw with the side of his hand. His pecker was still out of his pants. Bill looked at him.

"Blow me?"

Bill shook his head.

"Pull me?"

"No."

"Dang."

Bill thought that the thing to do now was kill Pete. Pete probably wouldn't remember he had been out here, but if he killed him, threw his body in the river, he wouldn't have that worry. Except there would be a dead body to fish out and it would obviously be murder. He could make it look like an accident, not murder. Maybe Double Buckwheat could end up taking the rap. He might be able to work that. Damn, you had a Siamese twin up for murder, were they both guilty? Could one rat on the other? Could you kill one and let the other live, saw off a head, have the other go around with one head and a cauterized stump?

Pete looked at Bill as if he had never seen him before, which was the way he looked at him every time he saw him, or anybody. For Pete, all days were new days. A nap was like a rebirth.

Bill, without saying a word, turned and walked back to camp. When he looked back, Pete was following. Bill went between two trailers, cut left, and went back to the Ice Man's trailer and stood for a moment on the steps. He could smell the river strong now, and it was unlike before. It was not the fresh clean smell of being born, but instead the old smell of dirt and decay.

Bill heard Pete tromping around the trailer in his direction. He slipped inside and locked the door. He listened with his ear to the door. He heard Pete come up on the steps and pull the handle. The handle popped back into place out of Pete's hand. He heard Pete say: "Blow me. You blow me, I blow you. Turns."

Bill took a deep breath and let it out as quietly as possible. He heard the steps creak and thought he heard Pete moving away. He went to the window beside the Ice Man's freezer, eased back the curtain and peeked out. Pete was staring back at the window over his shoulder. Bill was certain Pete saw him. Bill let the curtain drop slowly. He went over to the bed, kicked off his socks and shoes, lay down and looked at the ceiling. A few minutes later he got up and turned off the light and looked out the window and saw that Pete had turned and was facing the window, watching. It was if Pete had forgotten who he had made his blow job deal with.

Bill dropped the curtain, lay back down and looked at the ceiling some more.

185

I should have killed Pete, he thought. I could have killed him and maybe somehow fixed it so Double Buckwheat took the rap. I thought of that and I didn't do it. I think of things I should do and don't do, and things I shouldn't do, and those I do. It's the way I am. I wouldn't know a good choice if it bit me in the ass and hung on.

He got up and turned on the light and looked at himself in the bathroom mirror. His shirt was filthy where he had been crawling on the damp ground. And so was the front of his pants. He took his shirt and pants off and, wearing his underwear, he hauled them into the shower with him. He scrubbed his clothes with the bar of soap and scrubbed himself. He squeezed water out of his clothes and hung them up to dry on the shower curtain. He peeled off the wet underwear and twisted water out of them and hung them up as well. He dried off and went over to the window and looked out. Pete was still there, looking expectant. Bill went back to bed and lay there naked.

I need to go out there now, before daylight, and make Pete think I'm going to blow him, and take him down to the river and toss him in and let him drown.

No. I've done too much already. What I ought to do is get up there on the whirligig and screw those bolts back on with my fingers so they're tight enough to hold, that's what I ought to do. So far I haven't killed anyone. I've made some fuck-ups, but Chaplin killed that guy at the firecracker stand, and Mama died and I didn't report it, and the cop chased Fat Boy and me into the swamp and Fat Boy died of snake bites, then the deputy killed himself by accident, but I haven't killed anyone. No one.

Not yet.

I could stop all of this if I just go up there and fasten those bolts. Christ, I ought not to have loosened them in the first place. I should have stayed inside. I shouldn't have answered the door. I shouldn't have picked up that wrench, and I sure shouldn't have climbed up there to loosen those bolts. I shouldn't ever have laid down with that devil woman. I got time to correct things. I can go out there in a bit and climb up again and fasten those bolts with my fingers. I can do that. And I will.

So what? You don't help her, she'll get him anyway. It might not be the day coming, but it'll be some tomorrow soon.

Sure, that's right. But it won't be me doing it. I could even tell Frost. I could warn him. I could do all kinds of things and it wouldn't happen at all. I don't need her. I don't need anything she's got. But then I like what she's got. She's got plenty. She's got whatever it is, and she's got plenty of it, whatever it is.

The thing I ought to do is forget what she's got and go out there right now and tighten those bolts. That's right. Yeah, the bolts. I'll do that. The bolts . . . The bolts . . .

When Bill awoke it was to a scream and a clatter.

Twenty-eight

The fresh morning was bright and a little warm when Bill charged out of the Ice Man's trailer after having jerked on his pants and shoes. Glancing up at the whirligig, he saw the bucket had dipped down and it swung back and forth like a steam shovel scoop and little pops of fresh green paint were falling down from it like a slow radioactive rain.

Bill had never heard of Icarus, but the way Conrad lay, his neck bent, his back twisted in an even deeper U, his hind legs up in the air and drooping, balancing as if he were trying to do a trick by standing on his neck with his feet in the air, he had crashed in a way Icarus might have crashed after his wings melted from the heat of the sun.

Two gallons of bright green paint had exploded like a giant avocado all over the ground and Conrad. It had splattered onto the Ice Man's trailer, splotching the side of it as if someone had chewed and spat out great wads of spinach.

Some of the paint had spattered across the image of the Ice Man and had beaded up into fast-drying balls that looked like uncut emeralds.

A paintbrush, wet with paint, had flown onto the window of the Ice Man's trailer and had stuck there as if it were an exotic bird that had smashed into it. One of Conrad's shoes was lying upright in a puddle of paint.

Already there were others gathering. Pete, who Bill thought may have waited there all night for a blow job, and now, screaming, U.S. Grant, and a midget named Spike, spinning about on one leg uttering obscenities. Others were appearing: Double Buckwheat, pumpkin heads, some greasers, and finally Frost.

Frost and Bill moved toward Conrad at the same time. They arrived at his side at the same time. Conrad's head was turned and he lay with one side of his face in the dirt and the eye they could see was popped out of place on the tendons. It lay on his cheek as if trying to crawl off. There was green paint running down his long nose and over his top lip, gathering in the crease where his mouth was open, bathing a handful of teeth scattered inside his mouth. Another two or three teeth lay in a puddle of paint around his head. There was more green paint than blood, but there was blood too. Conrad was breathing in a rattling sort of way, like something fragile had been crunched inside of cellophane and was continually being unwrapped or danced upon.

Bill got down on his hands and knees and looked at the eyeball that was out of the socket so Conrad could see him. Above, the eyelash winked as if it still housed its charge.

"Fugged ub," Conrad said, spitting out teeth and paint.

"Oh shit, Conrad," Bill said.

"It'll be all right, Conrad," Frost said.

"Nuwont," Conrad said.

"God, Conrad," Bill said. "Jesus Christ."

"Uhtradta grubuhrailn. Dudnt mageid."

"Sure," Bill said.

"Uhtradto thunk rubba."

I bet, thought Bill.

Frost gently picked up the eyeball by the tendon and turned the eye so it could see him. "I'm sorry, Conrad."

"Yeg, bud dun'elp nun."

Frost lay the eyeball gently on Conrad's cheek. He turned and yelled at the spinning midget. "Call someone. Get my cell phone. Tell Gidget. Call someone. 911!"

"Uh feeg lig shid."

Conrad coughed a little, passed some gas in a hissing manner, and quit breathing.

"I was going to climb up there," Frost said. "I was going up there this morning. It was supposed to be me."

U.S. Grant, who had not spoken, but had stopped screaming, eased up slowly, fell to her knees next to Conrad. She took hold of him and lowered him so that he could lie on his side without his feet sticking up in the air. His extended eyeball became bathed in green paint, and now blood ran out from him in gluts and blended with it.

"He was going to surprise you two," U.S. Grant said. "He heard Bill say there was painting to do yet. A bucket left. He got the paint out of the car. He couldn't sleep because he wanted to surprise you."

"Jesus," Bill said.

"He climbed up there when daylight came. I was fixing him breakfast. He was going to finish and eat breakfast. I heard the bucket shift, and . . . He was going to finish up and eat breakfast."

"It's my fault," Bill said.

"No," Frost said, tears running down his cheeks. "It's my fault."

"That's right," U.S. Grant said. "Your fault. You had to have that rattletrap. No one but Phil knew how to really fasten it together. You had to have it though. And you had to have it painted right away. You always have to have things right away. He always wanted to please you, Frost. Always. We always want to please you, but you're not so smart. You fucked up. You and your goddamn idea."

"I know," Frost said. He reached out his hand and ran it through Conrad's paint-caked smattering of hair.

A blackness went over Bill. He got up and stumbled, fell down, got up, stumbled again.

As he groped his way toward his trailer, Gidget came out of the motor home. She had stopped to comb her hair and put on lipstick. She was wearing a pair of simple blue pajamas and a pajama top with a bright bird of paradise embroidered on the left side above her heart. She wore little blue house shoes with round blue cotton balls on the toes. She looked out at Frost and Conrad and U.S. Grant, then she looked at Bill, but she looked his way for only a moment, then she sighed deep, swallowed, took a deep breath, and went running out to Frost, screaming, screaming, as if it was she who had fallen.

Twenty-nine

U.S. Grant carried Conrad to her trailer and wiped him clean with paint thinner and paper towels, got his eye back inside its socket with the aid of tweezers and a couple of cotton balls and strip of Scotch tape.

It looked better than the other eye, which had met the ground and was like a grape stepped on by a size twelve. She cut a strip from her dress and made a string and patch from it, and after she cleaned him off good and dressed him in his red overalls, she tied the patch over the mashed eye and combed his wad of hair. She put both his shoes on him, then she wrapped him in a quilt.

Frost and one of the pumpkin heads carried the body from her trailer to the Pickled Punk trailer and placed him behind the Pickled Punks, on the floor pallet, next to a deck of cards, under the wrinkled picture of Jesus in pain.

Frost called the police then.

Inside the Ice Man's trailer Bill took the little stack of Westerns Conrad had given him and piled them neatly and arranged them by his bed in rows, then he restacked them on top of the Ice Man's freezer and sat on the bed and looked at them and tried to remember what each of them was about. He sat there until tears came, and then he shook his head and rolled onto the bed and cried and fell asleep to hide from the pain.

The police came out in a while, and they asked everyone out of their trailers and got stories from everyone, and they took names, and Bill gave a false last name that no one had heard before and had no reason to doubt. Down deep he wanted to give his real name and hope it meant something. He wanted to be taken away and punished.

The cops didn't seem to think there were any signs of foul play, even if the body had been cleaned up, and Pete didn't tell how he sucked a pecker and had seen Bill down by the river. Most likely he had already forgotten it. They only asked Pete a couple of questions, then decided it was a little like interviewing a turnip.

The police went away and Bill went back to his trailer wearing his guilt like a second skin. He was there fifteen minutes when he heard something outside. He pulled on his pants and went out barefooted. Frost was on a little step stool and he had a bucket of soap and water. There was a can of paint thinner on the ground. He was cleaning the paint off the trailer with a brush and a rag.

"Leave it alone!" Bill said. "Leave it alone!"

"Whoa, Bill, it's okay."

"Ain't nothing okay. Conrad's dead!"

"I know how you feel."

"You don't know shit. He ain't dead more than a few hours and you're cleaning the trailer."

"It has to be cleaned, Bill. We don't want Conrad's legacy to be green paint on the trailer and a brush stuck to the window. I'd rather not be reminded."

"Well, I want to be reminded. I want out of this whole thing. I'm sick of being in this trailer. I'm sick of the Ice Man. I'm sick of you. I'm sick of this goddamn carnival. You don't give a shit he's dead."

Bill went inside the trailer and slammed the door. A moment later Frost came inside and took a chair and sat with his hands in his lap, watching Bill lie in bed snuggling a pillow.

"Conrad meant a lot to me."

"Yeah. Tell me you raised him from a pup."

"You forget, Bill, when you first came here, you thought these people were retards, niggers, just freaks. It was I who told you different. I put you in this trailer for a purpose. I wanted you to be with the Ice Man."

"Well, I don't like him."

"You don't like how he makes you feel. Do you ever wonder why he makes you feel that way?"

"He don't make me feel any kind of way."

"Sometimes I think he's some kind of messenger for us all. That whatever each of us wants to see, we see it in him."

"That's silly."

"Could be. That little story I tell to the people who come to see him. I have to tell it that way, but it's not the truth."

Bill grew attentive in spite of himself.

"Do you know who Constantine was?"

Bill shook his head.

"A Roman emperor. He explored Jerusalem looking for holy locations where Christ had been. Where he had been crucified, where he had been buried. He claimed that the body lay in a church there. The Church of the Holy Sepulcher. Many believe it is still there, hidden away somewhere. Others believe it was never there. Some believe Constantine had it removed. He feared if anyone knew where it was, they might try to take it. Like the ark of the covenant, the body of Christ would have powers. Or at least people would think it did."

Bill slowly swung his feet to the floor and leaned forward.

"It is thought that the body was preserved with methods we no longer know. The body was hidden for fear it would be stolen, desecrated. Things changed in the Middle East. One upheaval after another. The body disappeared, or so some esoteric scholars claim. It is thought to have somehow found its way out of Jerusalem and to the United States. Was owned by an eccentric millionaire who also had the diary of the true Jack the Ripper, the severed dried head of John the Baptist, and Rasputin's penis, though his daughter disputes this and says she has it. And she certainly has something. It looks like a blackened banana. Anyway, that's not the point. A lot of money changed hands, it's said, and this millionaire bought the body of Christ. In time, the millionaire died, and somehow, perhaps one of his relatives, bitter for some reason, a nonbeliever, whatever, sold it to the carnival. This made it no less sacred. It allowed the Savior to be exposed to many people. I bought that exhibit and was told this story by the owner, but the story he gave out was the one I tell now. He said it was too much for people to know, or suspect that this was the true body of Jesus. Yet, when they viewed, he knew, somewhere down deep in their heart of hearts, they knew."

"I thought Christ was supposed to have risen. Ain't that how the story goes? That was true, wouldn't be no body."

Frost nodded. "If he was just a man, then there would be a body. He may not be the son of God, but he would still be one of the most important human beings to have ever lived. And if he was in fact the son of God, the body is his shell, not his spirit. It would have been his spirit that rose, not the shell."

"You're saying that . . . That's really the body of him?"

"I'm saying I bought the exhibit and the story. The body may in fact be the body of the previous carnival owner's kin. A bum who died and was preserved. It doesn't matter, Bill. Not really. It matters what you decide to believe.

"I'm going to go now, and I'm going to clean that mess on the side of the trailer. Then I'm going to try and find a place to have Conrad embalmed and buried. He was always a good and close friend to me, and now I intend to help him leave this world."

"He's already left it."

"I suppose he has."

Frost got up and went outside. A little later Bill heard him working alongside the trailer. Bill took the paperbacks off of the freezer and placed them beside his bed.

He got the hair dryer. He turned it on and blew away the frost. The figure inside didn't look much like most pictures of Jesus, but it did look a bit like the picture on the wall of the Pickled Punk trailer, but with eyes like Frost's. It had scars on its forehead, as if from thorns, and there were marks on its side, and Bill thought he could see some kind of mark on one of its feet. A nail wound?

Maybe it was just a wrinkle.

Thirty

Frost canceled the carnival that weekend and got permission to stay in that spot until he could take care of Conrad and have a time of mourning for himself and the carnival members. Most of them thought they ought to take the day Conrad went into the hole off and get back to work the next. They liked Conrad, some even loved him, but a buck was a buck, and you had to eat, one dead Wonder Dog or no. But it was, as usual, Frost's way or the highway.

It turned out things didn't go so slick for Frost. In town the body was held and it was insisted that next of kin be searched for. No one wanted to take Frost's word on the matter. Things like that had happened before, only to result in dire consequences for town officials. They put the dog on ice and Frost and the authorities started a search.

It turned out Frost was wrong. There was a cousin in Idaho. She was found easy. She wanted the body but was too much of an invalid to come down and get it. She asked if Conrad could be stuffed and a name plaque attached so he could be made into some kind of exhibit, and would this be easier for mailing? Frost lied and told her the body was too much of a wreck. She asked Frost to bring the corpse and, being Frost, he agreed. He wanted to be there to make sure Conrad went into the ground, not next to a door and an umbrella rack. He made arrangements to have Conrad embalmed and placed in a coffin from the animal cemetery, because those were the only coffins small enough to properly accommodate him and not have him rattle around in there during transit like a BB in a boxcar. It took two days for the embalming and fitting in the coffin, the one commonly used for collies and German shepherds. Frost had to go back the next day and load the coffin in the back of the station wagon and drive back to the carnival.

He came to Bill and told him about the cousin.

"I'm going to be gone for a while. I have to go to Idaho. It'll take me a week to get there, do the funeral, help out, and come back. You and Gidget are in charge."

"I don't know nothin' about being in charge."

"Others do, but they don't want it. Gidget's the one, but she'll need help. Little things. She'll tell you what to do."

"I could drive Conrad to his cousin's in Idaho."

"I have to do this, and for my sake, and Conrad's sake, I need you to help Gidget. Will you do it?"

Bill and Frost were standing outside the Ice Man's trailer. Bill walked over to the station wagon and looked in the back at the small blue coffin sitting on the old creased upholstery. Goodbye, my friend. Peace to you. And I'm sorry. But I can see that ditch coming and I don't even know how to steer.

*   *   *

Frost left that afternoon and that night, late, Gidget came to the Ice Man's trailer and scratched like a cat on the door.

"I know it's you," Bill said, then considered it might in fact be Pete come for his blow job.

"Let me in?"

"No. You go on."

"He's gone, Bill. We can be together."

"I killed my friend on account of you."

"It was on account of an accident."

"Wouldn't have been no accident without you and me."

"That's just it, Bill. It was you and me. Not me."

"No more, Gidget. Just leave me be."

"You want me, Bill. I know it. You know it."

Bill could see that ditch looming large.

"You let me in, let me take care of you the way only I can. You hear me, Bill?"

"I hear you."

"You let me in, honey, and I'll give you a taste like you haven't ever had."

"No."

"You're thinking about it—"

"No."

"—aren't you, Bill? You know what I can do—"

"Go!"

"—for you. It's not just what I can do, it's what you want. There's no use pretending you're worth something, Bill. You aren't. You're just like me, rotten to the core. You're tryin' to wear some kind of halo, like Frost wants you to. But that isn't you. You got any halo on, it's made of aluminum foil and a coat hanger, baby. You're who you are. You and me, we got rotten souls, and that's all there is to it. And there isn't anyone can make you and me happy, but you and me. Together."

"Please, Gidget."

"Bill. This is the last time I ask. I'm not one has to ask much, you know that. There are plenty out there ready and willing. Open the door."

When Bill opened the door Gidget leaped in, swung her fist and hit him over the ear and knocked him down and tried to kick him in the balls. He rolled and she caught his side with another kick. He got up and she kicked at him again, and he grabbed her foot and pulled her to the floor and jumped astride her and slapped her across the face, back and forth, back and forth, and she said, "Yeah, baby, yeah, do it," and he hit her again, and this time it wasn't anger, it was pleasure, and she shared the pleasure. She used both hands to grab the sides of her white blouse and rip it open, loosing braless titties on the world. Bill jammed his fingers in her worn-out blue jean shorts and tugged with all his might, ripping, exposing one beautiful thigh, then he ripped again, showing the rest of her. She scratched at him and ripped through his T-shirt and tore his flesh and he bled and she ran her hands over his chest, smearing the blood, poking the red fingers in her mouth to suck. He slapped her and she groaned. He tugged at his belt and she swatted his groin. He unfastened his pants, pushed them down, got on top of her. She tried to pull her thighs together. He bit her nipple and she spread her legs with a little squeak. She was hot and wet and sticky. He went into her and she said, "Have you now, you sonofabitch!"

* * *

And have him she did. Up one side and down the other. When it was over they lay together, she in the crook of his arm and he breathing heavy, feeling satiated.

"It didn't work out," she said. "It happens."

"It was terrible."

"I know. You lost a friend. We got the wrong one. We tried too hard. We got to know he's the one to get it, not hope he's the one."

"You won't give it up, will you?"

"It's bottom line, Billy. You either want me or you want Frost. Look here. We do this, we got the exhibit. You like the exhibit, don't you?"

"Sure. I like Frost too."

"Which do you like better?"

"Why have I got to choose?"

"You keep Frost, he's got the exhibit. Not us. Not you. You could be the man. You're dark at the middle, baby, but you do this, we get the thing, the dingus, then you and me, we're it, and you're the man. You're the driving force. Bad stuff is over. For good. I promise. This is for us. It's the best and easiest way to jump ahead in life. It's our jump, baby."

"He told me it's really the body of Christ."

"He tells people whatever they want to think about that thing, baby. He thinks he's some kind of do-gooder. He thinks he can rouse something good in you, and he'll do it with talk or he'll do it with that dead body. He's telling you it's Christ. Some other person he might tell it's the body of some rock singer. He feels you out, then tells you what he thinks will work. I'll tell you what I think it is. Something made of rubber."

"Well, I guess he didn't really say it was Christ. He said that was the true story he had gotten."

201

"He's got lots of true stories. I tell you it's just something rubber is all. He makes himself important with that thing."

"Hell, that's what I want. To be important."

"And you can have it. Listen, honey. Even if that was Jesus and he was here to help you personal, wouldn't work. You're rotten, just like I been sayin', but you want to pretend you aren't. You want to think maybe you can get religion or something to make you better, but once an apple is rotten, hon, it stays rotten. My advice is learn to be rotten and like it. There ain't nothing in that freezer's gonna change who you are, who anyone is."

They lay silent for a while. Eventually Bill spoke. "We did this . . . I don't want to start something. You know, a trend . . . Just this one time."

"What's that?"

"Something like this. Rotten or not. Just this one time. Right? I mean, there ain't no one else we want killed, is there?"

"When it's done, we'll just let it go. Believe me, it can be done. I just got to think about it awhile. We won't get in a hurry."

"Maybe if it was someone I didn't like."

"Listen here. He likes you, Billy. Really, he does. But he pities you. You want to be the source of pity? That's not true respect, friendship, or love. It's just what it is. I love you, Billy. I know how you and me are. I face the facts. But still, I love you. Do you really want me to keep lying down with a man with a hand on his chest? You really want me to give birth to a baby might have a hand on its chest, or coming out its ass or on top of its head? You really want that? You think about it. You think about how you've had me, baby. Ain't no one done the things to me you've done, ain't no one likes it the way we like it. I don't want to be shared. I want you."

"I still don't have anything against him."

"Who says you have to?"

Thirty-one

Gidget left him early, while it was still dark. She had gone out of there holding her shorts and shirt together with her hands, leaving him naked in bed. The bedclothes were torn, bloody in spots. He lay amongst their ruin thinking and seeing himself once again as the man on the stool, looking down on the Ice Man, giving the talk.

He had some random thoughts: Jesus. There ain't no Jesus. And if there was, this ain't it. He wouldn't end up in no freezer. And if he did, and this is him, what's that got to do with me? Frost pities me, like I'm another freak. He's the fuckin' freak. Telling me that bullshit about the Ice Man. Conrad, he was all right. I liked him. It shouldn't have happened, but it did, even if I didn't mean it. I didn't set out to hurt Conrad. It's not my fault. It's me and Gidget and that's all. Fuck Frost for telling me that story. Fuck me for ever thinking there was anything about that thing in the freezer. It ain't nothing but an exhibit I want.

Bill showered, cleaned up the bed, and dressed. There really wasn't anything to do that day, in spite of what Frost had said. They were locked in until word came from Frost. Gidget was supposed to keep things in order, but there was already an established order and she wasn't part of it, and he had no need to be part of it. Not until he had the Ice Man. Then he would for the first time in his life be important. Someone to reckon with. It might not be president of the United States, but it beat living off the leavings of your mother's checks. When she was alive to cash them anyway.

Around noon there was a knock on the trailer door and Bill answered it, hoping it was Gidget, but it wasn't. It was a dark-haired woman in blue jeans and a loose shirt. She was an attractive, somewhat large woman. She had a plastic trash bag in her hand.

"Conrad would have wanted you to have these," she said.

"U.S. Grant?"

"Formerly. I've lost the beard. I'm through with carnival life. I'm bringing all of Conrad's goods to you. This bag, that's the whole of it. Mostly cowboy books. He loved to read cowboy books."

"Where will you go?"

"Anywhere. I'm driving my rig out of here within the hour. I'm through. No beard. No work."

"It'll grow back."

"For now I'll shave it. Soon I'll get something done to it. I'll find work somewhere, even if it's banging oil field workers. I've had it up to here with this shit. I was thinking of leaving anyway. Now I've got nothing to keep me here. The whole thing's falling apart. Frost, he's losing control and I think it's that blond bitch's fault."

Bill took the bag.

"Well, good luck, Bill."

Synora, U.S. Grant, drove her cab and trailer out of there a half hour later and Bill never saw her again.

Thirty-two

A week went by and Gidget got a call on her cell phone that Frost had stopped in Oklahoma and had scoped out some new routes for the carnival and wouldn't be back for another week. It was a pleasant surprise. It gave Bill and Gidget more time together. They used it well. After that extra week, Frost came home.

The carnival packed up and things went back to the way they were, except they lost the half and half to a transvestite lover from Denton, and the midgets had grown surly in the extreme. Gidget did not knock on Bill's door, and at night Bill sat on his trailer stoop and watched the motor home, and some nights when the moon hit right, he almost thought he saw Conrad up there, lying down, riding out the rhythm of the couple below. But when he squinted, it was only shadows.

As for the rhythm, the rocking, there was plenty of that,

and Bill hated to know what was going on in there, Frost touching her with that dead leather hand in a black silk glove. He hated it, but he came out each night and watched for the rocking, and more often than not he saw it. He began to grit his teeth a lot and smoke cigarettes. He quit reading the books Synora had left, and on one fateful day when they were parked outside of Tyler, Texas, he took them all out and stacked them and set them on fire. From that point on, he no longer thought he saw Conrad on top of the motor home.

Some days he saw Gidget, but she never really looked at him. They had agreed on this. Agreed they had to not show any more than common courtesy between them. They were waiting for a moment. The exact right moment. But Bill thought sometimes she was too good at it, like maybe she had given up on him and was going to do what she planned by herself, leaving him out. The thought of this drove him crazy.

The summer rocked on and went away and fall came. The carnival made its new Oklahoma route, then dipped back to East Texas. A thing called El Niño, a kind of weather current, had, according to the meteorologists, messed things up. The weather was all haywire. There were floods and high tides on the West Coast of the U.S., hurricanes on the East. Water churned in the Gulf and washed the shores of Galveston with great violence. Wads of thunderstorms fell out of the sky at all times. Tornados tore across Texas. Near Corrigan, one even took away the whirligig, which Frost had never given up on, erecting it at each stop. The tornado carried the whirligig and one of the midgets around for a while, spat out the midget unharmed near a trailer park it didn't spare, knotted up trailers and whirligig together, and deposited them just off Highway

59 next to a car dealership, as if the tornado had created and was displaying a modern work of weather art.

Winter eased in and so did ice. Hail flailed the land and the trees cracked and bent. No one was really that interested in a winter carnival. Not now. In the old days when the weather was just cold they got business. But now everything was canceled. People were nervous and a little scared. They had never seen it like this.

Many things changed.

The whirligig was long gone and the other rides had slowly fallen into disrepair.

The midget who had ridden the tornado had finally given it up and left them to work at a filling station in Mineola, Texas. The remaining midgets had turned to shoving people about and using bad language freely.

No one ate breakfast at the table outside anymore. Too damn cold.

One of the pumpkin heads, a fella called Bim, just up and died one morning on the Texas side of the Red River, and had been buried in a pauper's grave in Paris, Texas, with nothing but his name on a cheap metal marker. Nobody wanted to stuff him, nobody claimed him. What he got was some dirt and a coffin so cheap it was pretty much a cardboard box, an appetizer for the worms.

Eventually the carnival, wounded from loss of personnel and morale, wound up at the spot where they had camped so many months previous. The spot where Conrad had fallen from the whirligig and the old Sabine roared by and the willows that hadn't washed away waved in the gale, clattering now with icy wind chimes. The sky was full of pearly clouds glazed with what looked like soap scum. Hail banged the cabs, motor homes, cars, and trailers like it meant business.

And while they waited here for the bad weather to pass, there were rumbles throughout the carnival.

"The Old Days are gone."

"Frost ain't what he used to be."

"I could make more money running a side show."

"I could do better with a shell game."

"I got some land, I can put up a sign. People would stop to look at me. And I could build a snake farm, get some Russian rats. Sew a fifth leg to a calf. Start my own business, stay in one place."

"Blow me?"

"Uh uh."

"Two heads better than one."

Pause.

"Okay."

Later.

"Now me?"

"Uh uh."

"Pull me?"

Whack!

Some rumbles different, some the same.

Bill and Gidget were still playing it careful, and Bill dreamed about Gidget and wondered if she dreamed about him.

The Ice Man, as always, lay silent.

Thirty-three

The carnival no longer buzzed. Frost paid money to the pasture owner so they could lay low by the Sabine for a while, and one day when it warmed a little and the ice melted, he became possessed with the idea it would be grand to perk spirits and order pizza from town for everyone. But when he called on the cell phone to order, no one would come out. He decided to send Bill and Gidget in for it.

Gidget, wearing her usual pissed-off look, the one that made you want to flatten her face, got in the car on the passenger side, and Frost, wearing only a T-shirt and light pants and slippers, stood on the ice next to Bill as if this were in fact his kind of weather.

"Get plenty pizza," Frost told Bill. "Morale is low. Mine included. A little thing like this can lift it. Don't get any of that stuff with little fishes on it. There's maybe one midget and some pinheads will eat it. It'll go to waste."

"All right," Bill said.

"Gidget's got the money. She's acting foul, but she always acts that way when you want her to do something. Don't pay her no mind. Thing is, I don't just want pizza, I want some time from her."

"All right."

"You doing okay, son?"

"I guess."

"Still think about Conrad?"

"Not much."

"I guess that's good. Not that we want to forget him, do we?"

"No."

"Well, you go on now, and be careful. Ice is starting to thin. I think today is going to be a hell of a nice day. Tomorrow, we move out."

"We got gigs lined up?"

"One a couple weeks from now. But we got to leave here tomorrow. That's all I'm paid up for, and the old man owns this land isn't generous or worried about iced-in freak shows. He doesn't care if we have to swim the river. He wants his money."

"Frost. That story you told me, about the Ice Man. It true?"

"I never said it was true. I said it was a story I got. Sometimes I believe it, and there are days I don't believe anything. But finally, in the end, you got to believe in something."

Bill nodded, unconvinced. He had wanted Frost to come out and say the story was true, that he believed it, that there was something miraculous going on that could change everyone's life. But he didn't. And there wasn't.

Bill took the keys and got behind the wheel. He backed out easy. As he turned the car around and made for the little road, he could hear ice crunching under his tires. Double Buckwheat, dressed in several shirts and a heavy coat and the bottoms to thermal underwear, wearing laced-up boots, was out by his trailer listening to rock and roll, dancing about.

"I wish that nigger would fall under the car," Gidget said.

"You're in a mood today," Bill said. They moved out of the field and onto the slippery road. The ice wasn't as melted as Frost had thought. It was hard, slow going.

"I'm just in a hurry, is all."

"A hurry for what?"

"You know."

"I figured that was done forgotten."

"No you didn't."

"Maybe I was kind of hoping it was forgotten."

"I don't believe that neither. We got our time now, Bill."

"How's that?"

"You heard Frost. Tomorrow we move out. Way we do it, is tonight you mess this car up. Nothing too weird, just undo a brake line."

"Cops will know right away."

"You haven't heard it all yet. You undo that brake line. You know how, don't you?"

"Sort of."

"Tomorrow, before we leave out, I'll say: 'Oh yeah, Bill says the brakes are going on the car. You ought not to drive it.' I'll throw a bit of a fit, like I'm trying to keep him from being hurt, you see. He'll like that. I'll get him to hook it up to the back of the motor home."

"What does that do?"

"He'll have to drive the motor home. I'll sleep in the back like usual, only I won't. He'll go up front to drive, and I'll tell him I'm taking a sleeping pill to get some rest, that I don't feel good. Whatever. I'll make up something. Before we leave I'll get out of the motor home and you slip in the back. I'll drive the Ice Man's cab behind him."

"You better make it farther back. He'll see you behind him in the mirror."

"I got a baseball hat, some sunglasses. I'll put my hair up and wear them. Unless he's looking for me, he won't know. What we're going to do is going to happen fast anyway and I got to be up front to do it."

"Sunglasses in winter?"

"This ice is uncomfortable to look at, has a glare."

"Yeah, all right. It does, don't it?"

"You're in the motor home, in the back. Frost will lead off. He likes to lead. I'll be behind you. That stretch of road back there, by the bridge. You know which part I mean?"

"Yeah."

"Before you get to the bridge there, there's a gap, land slopes off toward the river."

"I'm beginning to not like this."

"Just listen. What did you do as you came up on the bridge there?"

"I slowed."

"Why?"

"Because they've put in a bump there so you won't go jettin' across the bridge. I guess because it's narrow. They want you to stop and consider, watch for cars."

"Right. When he stops, you come out of the back and take him from behind."

"I prefer taking you from behind."

"Just shut up and listen. You put your arm around his throat, and you lock your hand in the crook of your other arm, and you use the arm that isn't choking like a lever behind his head. Like this."

She showed him.

"If you drop your elbow so it points out, you can choke the sides of his neck, cutting off the blood. He'll go out, but it won't strangle him. You start the motor home off the edge and into the water. Just ease it over there and go out the side door and I'll be behind you in the cab. No one behind us will be able to see what's going on, and I'll ease forward and nudge the motor home into the river. You come crawling up like you're exhausted."

"They'll see you nudge him."

"I'll stay back from you a ways, but when I see you're getting near the stop, I'll speed up, and soon as I see you go out the side there, I'll put on the speed. I'll be sure to be good and ahead of the others. All they'll know is I lost control, Frost did too, I bumped him, and he went under. No one will be expecting murder. That choke hold will put him out, but he could come around from it, see. Only thing is, he won't. The water will finish him. They look him over, they're not really looking for anything. There's no marks, you do it right. It'll just be a sad drowning."

"How do you know about a choke like that?"

"I've picked things up here and there. I had a boyfriend for a couple months was a judo instructor. They use that choke."

"You sure no one will see me get out of the motor home?"

"Say they do. It won't matter. It was going over the edge, you bailed out of fear."

"So I got to look like a coward?"

215

"You thought Frost was coming right behind you, then I hit the motor home from behind and he didn't have time."

"But I'm supposed to be driving the Ice Man's trailer. How do we explain that?"

"What's to explain? We're the only ones know about the switch-up. All we got to do is tell the cops you were sick and Frost and I invited you to lay down in the back, and I chose to drive the cab. I've driven every damn thing, have a license for it all, so nothing's suspicious about that. They won't think anything about me wearing sunglasses and a hat. That won't mean anything to them other than it's some kind of fashion statement."

"I'm so sick, how do I manage to get from the back and out the front door?"

"Tell it different then. He asked you ride with him. He'd been thinking about giving you more responsibility with the carnival. He wanted to talk."

They were nearing town now. The ice was more melted there. They drove over to the pizza parlor and went inside and made their order and sat at a table in the back on opposite sides sipping soft drinks through straws.

"And when he's dead," Bill said. "What then?"

"That's easy. You and me, baby. And we got the Ice Man. You like the Ice Man, I can tell that for sure."

"It's interesting."

"You'll look better giving that talk than Frost. And me, I won't have to deal with that hand anymore."

When Bill paid for the pizza it cost much more than he expected, and all he got back of Frost's money was a handful of silver.

Thirty-four

It was very cold that night under the car, and the wrench was small and Bill had to hold the little flashlight in his teeth. He didn't know if he should throw the wrench away afterwards or what, and he couldn't figure out the brake line anyway. He was lying there freezing, the wrench in his hand, the light in his teeth, trying to remember how this stuff worked. He finally realized it wasn't going to come to him.

A pale head poked itself under the car.

"What you doin'?"

It was Pete. He was bent down, looking under the car. It looked as if he were wearing his head upside down.

"Nothing. I'm working on the car."

"What wrong with?"

"I don't know."

"How fix it?"

"I don't know."

Bill slid out from under the car on the other side. He could feel the dampness soaking through his jacket, into his back.

"I'm supposed to get blow job," Pete said. He had risen up and was looking over the top of the car at Bill. He had on a thin coat.

"Yeah."

"I like it blowed."

"Good. Good for you."

"You blow me?"

"I don't think so."

"Then I blow you."

"No. I don't like it."

"No?"

"No."

Bill was uncertain what to do. He slipped the wrench in his coat pocket, held the flashlight and looked around. No one.

"I noticed the brakes weren't working right today. I thought I'd check them."

"You blow me?"

"I said no."

Bill went around, poked the flashlight at Pete for a better look, saw he had a big blue knot on the side of his face. His dick was hanging out of his pants.

Apparently, Pete had already tried to get his blow job tonight, but, as was the custom, he had failed. Only he'd forgotten. Probably, tomorrow, he wouldn't remember a thing about any of this. Then again, he might.

"I got to look under the hood," Bill said.

Bill popped the hood and poked around in there. He opened the brake fluid box and saw that it was full. He fastened the box up and closed the hood. "Looks low on fluid to me. I think it's leakin'.""

"I'm gonna git a blow job."

"You ought to go in. It's cold."

"Yeah. I'm gonna git a blow job."

"I don't think so."

"No."

"You already had it."

"Did?"

"Double Buckwheat. I seen you git it."

"Did?"

"Yeah."

"Frost not supposed to know."

"I wouldn't tell him. Who am I to come between a man and his blow job?"

"I had it?"

"Yeah. It's too cold for me. I'm going in. I'll see you, Pete."

"Okay."

As Bill walked to the Ice Man's trailer, Pete said, "Did I like it?"

Bill turned. "What?" Then he put it together. "Oh. Yeah. You thought it was great."

"Oh . . . Good."

"Good night, Pete."

Bill went inside the trailer. After a moment he looked out the window. Pete trudged across his view, and Bill went and opened the door and stuck his head around the corner. Pete was walking across the ground looking dejected. Bill watched until Pete came to the trailer he shared with assorted ill-shaped heads, and went inside.

Bill eased back in the trailer, got a tablespoon and a can of Coke out of his little refrigerator. Outside, he opened

219

the Coke and poured its contents on the ground. He went out to the car, lifted the hood and with the flashlight in his teeth again, he used the spoon to dip fluid into the Coke can. He filled the can, taking out most of the fluid.

He gently closed the hood.

Frost didn't poke his head out of the motor home.

Pete didn't show up asking for a blow job.

Double Buckwheat was nowhere in sight.

Neither midget, pumpkin, nor pinhead was stirring, not even a mouse. Bill took the can of fluid and the spoon over to the edge of the river and tossed the spoon way out for no other reason than he wanted to. He put his thumb over the opening in the Coke can and tossed it with a side arm move.

Fluid sprayed from the can, streamed out of it as it flew through the air, went into the water, churned under and was gone.

Bill watched the river for a moment, let out a breath, and went inside his trailer and sat down on the stool and used the flashlight and the dryer to look at the Ice Man.

He no longer slept with a blanket over it.

Thirty-five

Next morning, early, before time to go, Gidget woke Frost and told him about the brakes not working right the day before.

"I meant to tell you. I'm sorry. It slipped my mind. I woke up thinking about it and knew I had to tell you now, before things got to stirring. Bill told me to tell you yesterday, but I forgot."

Frost listened and patted Gidget on the back and went outside and lifted the hood. It was just light, but he could see well enough. He checked the brake fluid first thing. Gidget came out and stood by him in housecoat and house shoes, puffing frozen air out of her lungs.

"It's nothing," Frost said. "It's just low on fluid. I got fluid."

"You don't know that's all that's wrong. It could have a leak. It could be dangerous."

"Not at all."

"I will not have you driving that. I don't care what you say. Not until it's checked by an authorized mechanic."

"I always do my own work on the car."

"And you're not very good at it."

"You don't know that."

"Frosty, baby, if the weather weren't so bad, maybe I'd go with it. But with all this ice, I say hitch it up."

"It would be more dangerous pulling it in this weather than driving it, sweetie."

"I will not have you behind the wheel of that vehicle."

"You're serious."

"I'm serious. The ice isn't any better today. It's worse. And if you insist on driving that car, I will go back inside the motor home, and sit there. I don't feel well anyway. In fact, I feel pretty sick."

"What's wrong, honey?"

"I don't know. Nothing serious. A little bug. What would comfort me is if you would hitch the car, drive the motor home, and let me get some sleep. I could take a pill and rest."

"I don't like you taking pills."

"Now how often do I do that? I'm sick, Frosty. I don't feel good. You kind of wore me out last night."

Frost looked happy. "I guess I did. That was good . . . Was it okay without the glove?"

"Sure, baby. It was fine."

"First time you let me do that."

"You wanted to, I said sure, what's the deal?"

"It always bothered you before."

"I'm not so bothered now."

"I'm glad to hear that, honey. Really. I was beginning to wonder. I figured we had a kid, we had to get past that. I—"

"Frosty, I'd love to talk, but I'm freezing my tail off, and I don't feel good. You do what I told you, hear? I'd like to have you near me today. I just want to take a pill now and sleep, but I get to feeling better, I can come up there and sit with you."

Frost nodded. "That's the way you want it. That's how it'll be."

He closed the hood. He drove the car around behind the motor home, started hooking up the hitch. Bill came out of the Ice Man's trailer and walked around close to the side of the motor home while Frost was working. Gidget opened the door and Bill, looking to see if anyone was watching, slipped inside. "I'm going in," Gidget yelled back to Frost. "I'm cold."

"You do that, honey. I'll be inside in a bit."

Gidget slipped inside. Bill stood there with his hands hanging. "What now?"

"Hide in the bathroom."

"Give me some reason. It's been a while."

She kissed him hard. "Hurry."

Bill went through the bedroom and into the bathroom, got behind the shower curtain, and settled down in the tub. He lay there thinking about all the things that made this worth it. Gidget. The Ice Man. A position. Maybe his mother wasn't so smart after all. To hell with her and her piddling checks. To hell with that whole firecracker deal. It was Chaplin messed that up, not him. It wasn't such a bad plan, he just hadn't had the right people.

In the bedroom, Gidget slipped off her shoes and, still wearing her housecoat, got in bed.

*   *   *

223

Everyone was ready for Frost to lead, but he was slow about getting it together this morning. He wrestled with the trailer hitch and the car awhile. Finally, one of the midgets who had been vocal about the wait and had been known to bad-mouth Frost almost openly popped into his cab and, by means of a setup not unlike the one Conrad had used when he drove the Ice Man's trailer, bolted. As he drove by he showed Frost a face that spoke of resolution and rebellion. Here was a man determined to make his mark on the world, even if it was a greasy spot. Pete rode up in the front seat beside him. Pete still had a black eye and wore a wool cap pulled over his pin, like a sock tight over a highway cone.

When the midget charged by in a roar of mud and ice and mounted the road that led to the bridge, the others began to grow impatient. Horns honked and lights flashed. The idea of a wagon master had lost its appeal.

Frost finally climbed inside the motor home from the back and took a peek at Gidget.

Gidget lay in bed, feigning sleep. Her face was lineless, soft and sweet-looking as a baby's. Her hair was pushed back behind her ears, like a little girl about to play baseball.

Frost went through, slid the bedroom door closed, stopped in the bathroom. He took a leak in the commode.

Bill lay silent behind the shower curtain, listening to Frost drain himself. Frost flushed the commode, then Bill heard him washing his hands. Frost went out, closing the bathroom door.

In the bedroom, as Gidget heard Frost settle into the driver's seat with a squeak, she got up and pulled off her robe. Underneath she had on blue jeans so tight a pubic hair would stand out under them like a cable. She wore a long-sleeved black T-shirt. She dropped her feet into stringless shoes, pulled the ball cap out from under her shirt, put it on, slipped into her coat and went out the back door, closing it gently.

Gidget saw that everyone was watching her, so she walked quickly toward one of the cabs and slipped around front, between its hood and the rear of the Ice Man's trailer, hoping Frost had not heard her close the door or that he hadn't yet looked in the wing mirror and caught her walking away. She had counted on the fact he liked to settle in easy, fasten his seat belt, adjust the crotch of his pants, very methodically put the key in the ignition, check his gauges, then his mirrors. He was a creature of habit. Always the same way. Even in bed, always the same way. She stroked him, he stroked her, she sucked him, he sucked her, he mounted her and flapped his hand and finished. Every stroke was the same. She figured you counted them, there wouldn't be a difference of two or three strokes from one event to the other. He was like that. Ate a perfect amount of bran to make him shit a perfect little turd.

She slid around to the driver's side of the cab and hung on to the wing mirror, pulling herself up, almost hanging by her breasts. The driver was Potty, of the unclean fingernails.

"Y'all be careful today," she said.

Potty grinned his two teeth at her. Already he had beer on his breath and a look on his face like he'd like to strip Gidget and bend her over a sawhorse. Of course, every heterosexual male had that look when he saw her. Beside him sat one of the pumpkin heads. Gidget didn't know his name and really didn't care. The pumpkin head was playing with a defunct mosquito coil perched on the dash. The coil had been there for years, but it still had blacking on it, and the pumpkin head soon had the blacking on his face.

He always did that. Potty thought it was funny. He showed Gidget his two teeth and said, "You worried about me today, sweet thang?"

"Frost just wanted me to tell everyone to be careful."

"He's leaving without you."

"No. No he isn't. I'm driving the Ice Man's trailer."

"You gonna tell everyone to be careful one at a time, baby?"

She smiled. "Guess not."

She saw the motor home circling around in front of the Ice Man's trailer. She said, "Be careful now," dropped off and went around in front of the cab and along the right side of the trailer.

Potty turned to pumpkin head. "Hey, shit face. I think she's got a little thing going for me, don't you?"

The pumpkin head made a noise and dribbled some spit.

"You too, huh? Yeah. I think ole Potty may be driving the ole nail soon."

Potty knew this was bullshit, but it was something to think about.

Gidget got in on the passenger side of the Ice Man's cab and slid across the seat, turned the key Bill had left for her, pulled around quickly so she would be directly behind the motor home. As she drove, she pushed her hair up under her hat. She took sunglasses out of her coat pocket and slipped them on. She drove as close to the rear of the motor home as she could, a little to the right of the road, hoping Frost couldn't see her in the left wing mirror, and the right one would only show the right side of the cab.

Inside the motor home, Bill pushed back the shower curtain and slipped out of the tub. He went over to the bathroom door, and very gently opened it and looked out through the crack. He could see Frost behind the wheel. He saw the makeup mirror on the dash, and made it a point to keep the crack in the bathroom door slight.

Bill took a deep breath. His heart was thundering inside his chest so loud he feared Frost could hear it. There was a roaring in his ears. He didn't even think about turning back. He had to have that woman and he had to have the Ice Man. The thought of Frost with her another moment was more than he could bear. It wouldn't have mattered if God almighty had told him to stop now, he couldn't and he wouldn't. The very maw of hell meant nothing to him. He didn't fear that maw at all, the maw he wanted was the one Gidget would open up for him to let him go inside her until the moment it all came together and he was falling from on high into something sweet and wonderful that would finally turn to fire.

Frost began to slow down and Bill knew they were coming to the rise that lay in front of the bridge. He felt dizzy, so he took deep slow breaths, trying not to be too loud about it. The motor home slowed more, and then it was almost to a stop. Bill pushed the door open and came out of the bathroom quick and he could see as he went that Frost had spotted him in the makeup mirror, and Frost was about to turn, but Bill didn't want that. He didn't want to see the face straight on, the mirror was bad enough. He leaped forward and brought his elbows down on Frost's shoulders so he couldn't move, and Frost said, "Bill," but Bill didn't answer. He slipped his left hand around Frost's neck, but Frost automatically dropped his chin so that he didn't really have the throat at all.

Frost had one foot on the brake, and as Bill tried to choke, tried to adjust his arm, Frost pushed down on the brake harder, so hard Bill heard the bones in his leg snap.

Bill put his fingers in Frost's nostrils and pulled up and Frost let out a noise, and Bill's left arm slid into place, and now he put his left hand into the crook of his right elbow and put his right hand behind Frost's head, and with his elbow pointed forward, he began to push with his right.

Frost wasn't easy. Frost was strong. He came up out of the chair with Bill hanging on him, but his leg was gone and he couldn't stand. He fell back down in the chair. The motor home rocked forward against the rise in the road, held. Frost pushed up on his good leg and tried to swing his bad leg out and around the chair, and as he did, Bill jumped up and locked his legs around Frost's waist and fell backwards, and now they were rolling on the floor, Frost trying to reach back and get hold of Bill, but not having any luck about it.

The motor home banged forward suddenly, over the bump, almost on the bridge, then it veered to the right and began to slide as if on butter-greased canvas. They were being pushed from behind.

"Not yet!" Bill screamed, as if he thought Gidget might actually hear him. There was another bump and this time the motor home went right, and then it was falling off the gap between bridge and land. It skimmed the bank with its tires, then hit with a smack and the car fastened to it rose up its rear and flapped down and hung its back tires briefly on land.

When it stopped Bill was lying against the windshield with his arm still around Frost's neck, and he could see water. The motor home was going under. Frost had quit fighting, and Bill let go of him. The motor home righted itself and floated, but the car that it had been dragging was pulled completely away from the bank and then its weight took it under and it made the motor home's rear end dip.

Bill caught the driver's seat and held as the front end went up. He saw Frost, unconscious from the choke, slide back and into the bedroom door, his bad leg bent up and behind him like a broken green stick. Bill scrambled to the front door and jerked it open and jumped out into the water.

The water was all the cold needles in the world and they stuck into him and he went mindless for a moment and could not decide if he was dead or alive. He rose up, his knees on something firm, and when he looked down it was the windshield of the motor home, and through it, inside, he saw Frost spinning around and around in the water with his mouth open, his eyes seeming to look at him, his arms spread wide, his destroyed leg wrapped around his good one.

The motor home went out from beneath Bill and sucked him down. He rolled back with the agitation of the river, and in that moment he saw the Ice Man's cab and trailer up by the gap in the bridge. The cab was poked out over the edge of the road, nodding toward the water, and he could see Gidget trying to scuttle out the window, but the trailer itself was sliding slowly over the ice behind her. It was jackknifing in slow motion. The trailer swung completely around, scraped along the bank, dipped its ass in the water and dove, pulling the cab after it.

It was then Bill knew Gidget hadn't panicked and pushed too early, but had meant to kill him and Frost both while she had them together. She had meant to do it all along. But it hadn't worked out just right. The trailer had betrayed her, dragged her down with them.

A weakness went over him worse than the cold and the water. The water churned him about and lashed him and brought him under, and when he rose up on the crest of a brown hill of foam, Gidget's baseball cap charged by him

229

in a wad. Then he saw that somehow the trailer had gone down and back up with the ass end pointing toward him. The end tipped slightly forward and there was a blasting sound and the back of the trailer ripped open, and the freezer containing the Ice Man, having gotten whipped about and come loose, had sent its weight through the back wall of the old trailer and now it hit the water like a cannonball and rode up on the rolling mounds of water and gained momentum, bouncing up and down.

The trailer's busted rear end filled with water and it slid beneath the river with a thirsty gulp. Up on the bridge Bill saw the cab and trailer driven by the guy called Potty. A pumpkin head was standing outside the cab pointing at the water. The water rolled and he lost sight of them.

Bill was brought under and up a dozen times, coughing for air, losing sensation in his body, and as he went around a bend in the river, pursued by the freezer, he saw the wet blond head of Gidget bob out of the water, and he saw her washing toward him, swimming frantically.

Thirty-six

Bill was raked along the bank and he tried to grab it and get up on it, but the river wasn't having any of that. He finally got his arm twisted into some roots and they held. When he looked up, Gidget was washing toward him. He tried to lash out at her with his good arm, but he missed her, and her body slammed against his and she swung over and grabbed the same roots he was holding. The roots slowly began to rip loose from the bank.

"Bitch!" he screamed. "Bitch!"

She reached out and raked his face with her nails, and suddenly there was a shadow. He and Gidget turned. It was the freezer bearing the Ice Man, and the bend of the river had propelled it, like them, toward the bank with tremendous speed.

Gidget kicked off of Bill with her foot and the freezer slammed against Bill and when it popped back, Bill was pushed way into the mud of the bank, one arm clinging to the roots, his face a ruin. Bill's hand slipped and he went under. He was barely aware of being alive. The water swirled him along the bottom, and he reached out with his one good arm and tried to clutch on to something out of reflex, and did. It was something heavy and it wasn't attached to anything. He churned along the bottom with it in his hand, and as the river filled his lungs, he knew, and found almost amusing, that what he had grabbed was the wrench he had tossed so long ago. The wrench that had sent Conrad to his death. He tried to laugh out loud and the water filled him and finished him and took him away.

The freezer coursed on and the roots Gidget was holding broke loose and she washed after it, grabbed it, and with hands so numb she could hardly feel them, pulled herself on the bobbing freezer and straddled it. The force of the water and all the banging and twisting about had ripped her tight blue jeans until they were nothing more than blue bands around her calves. Her T-shirt was washed up over her back.

She put her face to the glass. She could see the Ice Man in there. He had been knocked about, and lay on his side, his head turned as if to look at her with one eye.

Up on the bank two old men had backed their pickup close to the water and were out illegally dumping their garbage in the river. They were pulling bags of trash out of the truck one at a time and tossing them in the water, telling each other stories about things they had done.

They saw the freezer and the blonde go by. One of the men, a black plastic bag of trash in his hand, said, "Goddamn, Willy, I can see her ass."

"You betcha," said the other.

Gidget floated rapidly on down and away, the two old men watching until she made a turn in the river and was twisted out of sight.

PART FIVE

A New Climate

Thirty-seven

So, you just sort of slipped on the ice and ran into the motor home?"

"Yes. It's all my fault."

"Naw. Naw. It happens."

The sheriff poured Gidget another cup of coffee and made to adjust the blanket, trying to steal a look at the front of the wet black shirt, the two nipples poking at the fabric. As he moved the blanket, Gidget shifted in the chair and crossed her long legs. The blue jean pieces still clung to them. Her legs were coated with dirt and little bits of sticks and leaves, but she looked all right to him.

"This your carnival?"

"My husband's. I'm afraid it's all over now. I don't want anything to do with it. Jesus, not after . . ."

"The other fella?"

"He worked for my husband. They were supposed to discuss business. It's all my fault. Jesus. Did they find him?"

"Not yet. And it isn't your fault. It's the weather's fault. You remember that, little lady. It's the weather. You're not responsible for anything."

"Thanks, Sheriff . . . I can't thank you enough."

"Don't thank me. The river's to thank."

"I don't remember much."

"It washed you and that freezer up near a fish camp. You was clinging to that freezer like nobody's business. Couple niggers seen you and brought you in. By the way, that two-headed nigger. That real or some kind of made-up thing?"

"It's real. He's a Siamese twin."

"I didn't think that stuff was real. This freezer, we got it out back. That man in there. That a real man?"

"I don't think so."

"That could cause some problems."

"Listen, Sheriff, you got to do what's right, but my husband bought that thing from another carnival. He's had it for a long time. It's just an exhibit. If it was ever anybody it was somebody long ago and ain't nobody to anyone now."

"We ought to take fingerprints."

"I know. And you can. But I'm telling you. It ain't nothing to nobody but me. If it gets confiscated, I wouldn't have any way to make a living."

"Then you're going to keep the carnival?"

"No. Just the exhibit, if you'll let me."

Gidget moved her shoulder slightly and the blanket slid off and showed not only her nipples against the shirt but more of her long legs and the bottoms of her buttocks.

"I'd do almost anything to keep from the red tape, Sheriff."

"Yeah?" the sheriff said.

"Yeah," Gidget said, and pushed the blanket completely off and let it rest on the back of the chair.

The sheriff went over and locked the door.

Thirty-eight

Bill's house wasn't hard to find, even by moonlight. He had given her a good description. Across from it was a clapboard shack that had once housed a firecracker stand.

Gidget parked the van she had bought in the backyard. She had purchased it with savings Frost had kept in a bank in Enid, Oklahoma. The freezer sat in the rear of the mini-van, housing the Ice Man without electricity.

Gidget slipped on gloves, got out with a crowbar, and worked up the back window of the house. When she slid the window open a smell came out that made her swoon. She took deep breaths and went back to the car and got a handkerchief, put it over her nose, and climbed through the window.

Inside, Gidget moved her flashlight around. The bed in there was black with something greasy. She moved over closer and the smell got worse. It was not only a dead

240

smell, but a sweet smell, like decay and sugar boiled to-gether.

In the light of the flash Gidget could see there was a skull bathed in the black goo. Gray hairs were twisted about at the top of the skull. The corpse had been wrapped in trash bags at one point, but rats had gotten into it and ripped them open and exposed the body and eaten parts of it.

Gidget went into the living room. She poked around for thirty minutes before finding a desk drawer with the old woman's checks in it. She poked around some more until she found an old checkbook and some things with Bill's mother's signature on them.

She put the copies of the signature and the checks in the coat pocket and went out the way she had come, closed the window.

She checked the mailbox for grins. Someone had stuck a phone book in there.

She tossed the phone book back inside the mailbox and drove away.

Thirty-nine

After a few months the weather got good and warm and the insurance policies Frost had taken out on himself naming her the beneficiary came through. She cashed the checks at a bank in Tyler, Texas, on a hot day in July. She had already forged the old lady's name and managed to get those checks cashed at a pawn shop in Beaumont. She hadn't gotten the full of the money, but the pawn shop hadn't asked questions. She had worn a black wig during the process and had glued some small, but obvious, black hairs to her upper lip. Under her dress she had slipped her slim waist through a couple of old rubber inner tubes she had purchased at a junkyard. The pawnbroker might remember her, but he would remember a fat black-haired lady with a light mustache, not a blond bombshell.

A few days later she drove by a place in Nacogdoches where she had seen some wetbacks sitting on a curb wait-

ing for gringos to offer them work. There was a nice-look-
ing young Mexican there when she drove up.

"Job?" she said.

"Sí."

She motioned for the young man to get in. He did. He
rode in the passenger seat, stealing looks at her legs, which
were long and brown in khaki short-shorts. Her hair was so
blond he wondered how it matched the other spot.

He looked back over his shoulder and saw the freezer in
the back where the rear seat used to be. He assumed she
needed help unloading it. She drove him out in the country to a little house she had rented. She had the young man
help her slide a piece of plywood up to the back of the van,
then slide the freezer down the plywood into the yard. The
young man started when he saw what was inside.

"Okay," she said. "You understand okay?"

"Sí . . . But not okay."

"Sure it is." She reached in the pocket of her shorts and
took out a hundred dollar bill and gave it to him. "Okay?"

He thought maybe it was okay.

She went in the house and came out with a hammer. She
broke the glass on the freezer. The smell inside was wet,
but not foul. It smelled like damp straw. She pointed to the
Ice Man and made some motions. The young man swallowed, thought about the hundred, looked at those long
legs of hers and that big smile. He took the hammer and
tapped out the rest of the glass, got hold of the Ice Man.
The body was like a log. It was very heavy. He pulled it out
and it didn't flex or move.

He followed her, carried the log of a body to the falling-
down garage. Inside were two sawhorses. She had him get
the plywood and put it over the sawhorses for a table. She

gave him an electric saw and strung some extension wire from the garage to the house.

She came back and picked up the saw and made a sound with her tongue that was worth watching her make and was meant to sound like a saw. She waved the saw at the Ice Man.

"No," the Mexican said, and shook his head.

Gidget pulled another hundred from her pocket. The Mexican looked at the hundred hungrily, sighed, relaxed.

He took the hundred and put it with the other and took the saw and cut off the petrified man's right foot. There was a thing in the corner with a chute on it and it was already plugged up with an extension cord. She pointed that he should put the foot in that. She turned on the switch and he put the foot inside and there was a mechanical gnawing. The foot came out in chips and dust on the ground. The woman stood back as he did it, as if she might accidentally touch the thing and somehow be poisoned.

"It was made by an artist in Cisco, Arkansas," she said.

The Mexican, not understanding, gave her a quizzical look. She laughed and showed her nice teeth.

He smiled.

"If you spoke English," she said, "I would give you a bit of advice. Insurance money is better than a wooden man any day. A real man for that matter. Do you hear me, handsome?"

The Mexican looked at her and smiled.

"You're so polite. You want some pussy, don't you?"

He grinned some more and went back to work.

When the Mexican was finished, Gidget had him shovel up the chips and dust into a black plastic bag and twist it closed with a wire tie. She invited him in the house and gave him a drink. Before the day was through she had him in the shower, then the bed. For the rest of the day the Mexican wore an expression that said he thought he had fallen into the most wonderful gold mine in existence.

Next morning they left out of there, abandoning the house, the freezer, the chipper, and sawhorses. She drove. The Mexican sat in the seat next to her, the black plastic bag with the Ice Man's chips and dust in it behind them on the floorboard between front and middle seat.

They drove across Texas for a long full day. It was very hot and she liked to drive with the air conditioner off and the windows down. The air made him sleepy. The back of his neck was damp and his flesh stuck to the seat.

Just outside of El Paso they hit a long stretch with no traffic behind them. She made it clear to him she wanted him to open the bag and let its insides out.

He opened the bag and held his upper body out of the car window and shook the bag and let what was in it blow away. He watched the chips and sawdust take to the hot wind, swirl across the dry Texas landscape and mix with the heat waves and the dust from the van's tires. Finished, he let go of the bag. It fluttered down the empty highway behind them, a black plastic spirit flying away.

When he turned back inside, Gidget looked over at him. She was wearing sunglasses, but he could see her eyes behind them, and at the same time he could see his face in them. She smiled and turned back to the highway.

The Mexican looked where she was looking, saw a dead animal of some kind in the road, saw a host of vultures rise up from it with a violent burst of dark wings.